Rimshot's Hard Target

Bad Boys of Beta Squad series, Book 2

Siobhan Muir

ISBN: 1-947221-10-8
ISBN-13: 978-1-947221-10-9

DEDICATION

Dedicated to the missing and the families and friends who never gave up hope they'd be found.

ACKNOWLEDGMENTS

Writing a book is never really a one-person job, and writing a series is especially difficult alone. Keeping track of details is so much easier when you have help. Not only does it take a great deal of hard work, editing, and research on the part of the author to get things correct, but without my compatriots, there'd be a lot more mistakes. Huge thanks to Cat Johnson for offering me this opportunity to join my SEALs with hers. I fangirled over her back in 2012 at Authors After Dark and I'm still doing so now that she's invited me to play in the big girls' pool. Great thanks go to Silver James who made sure the typo bugs weren't too big and the story made sense from start to finish. Thanks to Emily Drew who gave me superb copy-edits. Those typos and missing words are everywhere! Thanks to Kris Norris for redesigning the cover to fit the second printing.

CHAPTER ONE

"To Bronco and Lindsey."

Chief Kevin "Rimshot" Stanton raised his pint with the other members of SEAL Team 9, Bravo Squad, affectionately known as Beta Squad. He tried to smile, but he worried it came out more as a grimace.

He swigged his beer to wash down the bitter taste in his mouth. John "Bronco" Andrews had retired from active duty. *Effective today.* Kevin had lost a damn good teammate as well as a friend. Bronco had been his spotter for more ops than he could count, and while he'd heard they'd get a new teammate, no one could replace Bronco.

Bronco's retirement, on top of Ghost's debilitating injury and his sister's disappearance over fifteen months earlier, put the cap on a particularly craptastic year. None of Kevin's searching had done a damn bit of good to find Bethany, even the one time he'd gone home to Kentucky. She'd disappeared off the face of the Earth, and no one could find her.

Kevin forced his hand to relax around his pint glass before he shattered it in frustration. His *venerable* father sent in a special ops group from the army with the acronym SNAIFU, and even they had no luck. *Probably because of their name.* They'd come up empty and fifteen months had passed. No movement of any kind had happened and Kevin was ready to go AWOL and hunt for her himself.

"Damn, Rimshot. You look like you got a gut full of buckshot." Chief Todd "Magic" Hunter shook his head as he clinked glasses with Kevin. "What's got your tail in a twist?"

Something about a Texas drawl could drag a smile out of Kevin. He'd known his share of good ole boys in Kentucky, but Texans had it down to a science. Magic only hammed it up when he meant to calm his teammates down.

"Nothing. Just sucks that Bronco's retiring. He's been in this squad longer than any of us." Kevin didn't say the word *survived.* Attrition in the SEAL ranks happened no matter how well trained they were. No one could outrun death when it came calling.

"Yeah, well, you heard his reasons. He's been here a long time and he wants time with Lindsey." Magic sounded a little wistful now that he had his own wife. "No one can doubt his service to his country, though, and he's getting out before the chance is gone. Can't say as I blame him."

Kevin didn't blame Bronco, either. But he did wonder what the hell the old man would do now. *What would I do if I retired from the SEALs?* The answer came back with blinding clarity. *Find my sister.*

Lt. Jim "Retro" Waters sidled up to them and scanned Kevin's face. "All right, who needs killing and where do we find them?"

Kevin snorted. "No one needs killin'. As far as I know right now." He raised an eyebrow. "We get new orders, LT?"

"Not that I've heard, but you look like someone shot your dog, so I figured I'd ask." Retro narrowed his eyes and tilted his head. "What's going on, Rimshot?"

Kevin shifted his gaze to Bronco and Lindsey, laughing with some other guests. He slipped into his

Samurai Mask, the face he wore when killing and when he needed to secure his emotions.

"Bethany's still missin'. No word."

"Fuck." Retro's jaw clenched and his gaze swung toward Lt. Chris Hunter as if seeking an anchor in turbulent seas. He'd learned what it was like to lose someone he'd cared for when she'd been kidnapped.

"Aw, hell, Rimshot. I'm sorry." Magic lost his humor. "Who'd they send after her?"

"The Army."

"What?" Retro looked like he's swallowed his tongue. "You serious? The Army?"

"Yeah, some special forces group called SNAIFU."

Magic snorted. "There's a group called snafu out there?" He shook his head. "What's it really stand for?"

Kevin took a swig of beer. "Don't know, don't care." Truth was he didn't want to tell them. It was too farfetched. "The upshot is they didn't find my sister."

"Why didn't your dad send in the SEALs?" Retro growled.

"She disappeared on American soil. SEALs don't operate domestically."

"Where?"

Kevin bit back a curse and set down his glass. "On the old man's estate."

"Are you fuckin' kiddin' me?" Magic gaped. "He lost her at home?"

"Yeah."

"Doesn't he have security? Cameras and dogs and shit?" Retro crossed his arms over his chest.

"Yeah." Kevin had spent many a day skirting and deceiving the cameras to escape his father's political life. "But in that part of the estate, it's too overgrown and there's somethin' fuckin' with the cameras. No one saw her come or go. All they found was her horse."

"Have you been home since?" Magic asked.

3

Kevin shook his head. "It was an election year, and he lost. The old man is still on a rampage and he might not consider us family, but he's thorough when it comes to looking for his possessions."

Chris limped over to them, pushing between Retro and Magic. "Did I hear you right? Does your father consider your sister one of his possessions?"

Old anger churned in Kevin's gut as he nodded. "Yeah. To him, that's all women are good for. They're meant to look elegant on your arm and be brood mares. Hell, he values his quarter horses more than he did my mother or sister."

Chris's expression hardened. "Sounds like a real charmer."

"Yeah, well, he was a senator and a career politician. Charm is woven into his suits." A grin washed quickly across his lips. "But he never convinced my maternal grandfather. I think Granddaddy saw right through his sweet talkin'. That's why he left the bulk of his money to me and my sister. Senator Stanton can't touch a cent of it."

The ingenuity of his grandfather still made Kevin laugh. The old man had watched his daughter's marriage with suspicion that only grew over the years. He made it very clear he wanted all the money meant for his daughter to go to her children. He'd always had time for Kevin and Bethany. Besides his sister, Granddaddy had been the only other family member cheering Kevin's choice to join the SEALs.

"Are they still looking for your sister?" Chris had always kept up with the personal lives of her men, even after she came off active duty.

"Yeah, I think so. It's been fifteen months so the rush has died down." There were other reasons for that, but he didn't need to share them here. "I gotta do something, but when I went home on leave, I didn't find shit. And the powers-that-be ain't sharin' intel."

"Sounds like you need someone who specializes in missing people." Chris glanced at her husband and Retro before fixing Kevin with her direct stare. "My friend Jaime Hensen, the Maid of Honor at my wedding, is a private detective who finds those thought to be lost forever. She's a cold case expert and never gives up. Plus she has police contacts all over the U.S. and some abroad, too."

Immediately, the image of a sassy auburn-haired woman with a star map of freckles across her nose filled Kevin's mind. She'd been dressed to the nines at Chris and Todd's wedding, and nothing could curb his hard-on that whole night. He hadn't slept with her. *More's the pity.* But he'd spent most of the evening listening to her talk, enjoying her scent and her honey-colored eyes.

"Yeah?" He hid the rising anticipation with a look of disbelief. "What can she do that the U.S. Army can't?"

"You want a list?" Chris smirked and Kevin snorted with rueful agreement. "Just give her a call." Chris jotted a phone number down on a scrap of paper. "She really is remarkable at finding people, alive or dead, and she never gives up. She definitely has the heart of a SEAL."

Kevin blinked and stared at Chris, scanning her face. *How does Chris know anything about my heart?*

It took him a few seconds to realize she referred to Jaime's determination, not his own pining for her best friend. *And I'm not pining for her.* No, not at all. In fact, it had been a whole week since he'd thought of her.

Most of which we were in training.

"Thanks, Ghost. I'll take a look." He pocketed the card as he nodded.

"Hey all, thanks for coming again. We have one more announcement."

Kevin and his four teammates refocused on Bronco, banging against his glass for their attention.

"Oh, God, it's not a new security company you're heading up, is it?" Petty Officer Third Class Eugene "Deli"

Rubenovich rolled his eyes. "You guys heard about GAPS, right?"

Bronco snorted. "You looking for a fall-back position when you retire from the Navy, Deli?"

Everyone laughed.

"No, I got an even more important job lined up." Bronco shared a satisfied grin with his wife. "I'm gonna be a dad."

"What?"

"Hooyah! Way to go, Bronco."

"Congratulations, Lindsey." Chris crossed to Bronco's wife and hugged her.

Other cheers and congratulations echoed around the room, but Rimshot's gut sank. *Damn, he's really out of action now.*

"Damn, Bronco. You sure you're up for that?" Chief Petty Officer Greg Killian smirked, his eyes glittering with barely suppressed rage. "Scarier than a marriage."

Bronco laughed off the unpleasant undercurrent from Killian. "Don't see as I got a choice now, but yeah, Bam-Bam, I'm kinda looking forward to being a daddy."

Killian's smirk turned sour, but he raised his beer and toasted them while the rest of the crowd went on to congratulate the expectant parents. Deli shot Rimshot a grimace and shook his head. *Bam-Bam's been a fuckin' mental case since his wife cuckolded him.* Oh, Killian had gotten the job done, but he'd been surly as hell. The squad rarely saw him outside of training or ops anymore.

The party wound down after that and Kevin said his goodnights before he got too maudlin to drive his ass home. He wished Bronco and Lindsey well, but he couldn't understand their happiness. *If I've ever found it, it was in the Teams.* The Navy accepted him and didn't care where he'd come from or how much money he'd had. When he'd turned his back on his father's political aspirations for him, his father had threatened to cut him off from his inheritance, an inheritance the senator had no control over.

Kevin snorted as he slid behind the wheel of his blue Toyota Tacoma. *You can't live on a Navy wage.* The distain in his father's voice still rang in his head after all these years. *Suck my dick, sir.* Senator Stanton couldn't understand what it was like to live on something he'd earned rather than been given. Kevin preferred his way of life.

He threw the truck into gear and headed toward his apartment, shoving his father's issues to the back of his mind where they could be forgotten again. He didn't have time to wallow, he still had to figure out a way to find Bethany.

Fifteen fuckin' months and no sign. If he believed in conspiracies, he'd think one had taken his sister. But there'd definitely been a cover-up of some kind. He'd checked with a few of his Army buddies from the Rangers, and they said something had gone wrong with the special forces sent in. No one was talking, but scuttlebutt had it the commanding officers disappeared along with his sister.

Kevin pulled into his parking spot and threw himself out of his truck. The night air was too warm for January, even in Coronado, but it would give him a chance to run off his frustration. He jogged up the steps to his apartment and unlocked the door, barely restraining himself from throwing a punch at the wall. He tossed his keys onto the kitchen table and the card Chris had given him fluttered to the floor.

He crouched and picked it up, reading the name and number again. Jaime Hensen, the sexiest woman at Chris's wedding, and private investigator. He shot a look at the clock on the microwave. Too damn late to call her tonight, but he could call her first thing in the morning. His cock liked the idea, but he quelled its antics as he focused his mind on an emotion-clearing run around base. He needed her to do a job, not a 'blowjob'. Maybe he'd throw himself into the Pacific to work out some of his frustration and cool the sexual interest still plaguing him since the wedding.

That would be a helluva cold shower. Kevin headed for his bedroom to change. *Cold night run it is.* Traditional for being a SEAL, and running off aching blue balls. *Works for me.*

CHAPTER TWO

Jaime stepped back into her home, sweat streaming down her back under her hoodie. She didn't particularly like running, but she found the constant exercise emptied her mind of all her stresses and cleared the way for solutions to any problems she faced. Like the problem of the missing boy from the Navy family just down the way from her. Mom was deployed on an aircraft carrier and dad had his hands full with a set of two-year-old twins. He'd turned his back on his six-year-old son for just a moment or two and the boy had disappeared.

It had taken Jaime almost a week to track down leads to mom's sister, a woman who had a beef against the Navy and had lost a young child. She'd been in town, but hadn't told her sister or brother-in-law, and when she saw the opportunity have a child in her life again, she took it. Jaime rolled her head on her shoulders, trying to loosen up the stress-tightened muscles. At least the boy was back with his father and auntie was in a psych ward.

Jaime scrubbed her face as she headed for the shower. *I'm never having kids.* Too many whack-jobs out there to worry about children. And she'd seen most of them in her job. The idea of them getting their hands on anyone she cared for made her sick to her stomach. *Probably the same sort of bastard who took Mia.*

The reminder of her missing sister made her throw off her hoodie and strip down to wash away the sweat and memories. She hated remembering why she became a private detective, but took solace in having saved so many parents the heartache she still carried. *I will find you, Mia. I promise. Dead or alive, I won't give up on you.*

She turned on the shower and stepped under the spray before the tears could make their usual appearance. Mia had been missing for over twenty-two years, but Jaime hadn't given up. *Fool.* But she couldn't do that to her older sister. She continued to search in her spare time, hoping to discover one clue, one piece of evidence to crack the case. *If I ever find it, I'll probably hit the ceiling...just before I lose my voice from screaming.* Yeah, it wouldn't be pretty, but it would bring her some relief and satisfaction.

Jaime finished her shower and toweled off, grateful the bathroom mirror was fogged over. She might have hidden her tears in the spray, but her face would give her away. She wiped the last of the moisture off just as her phone jingled from the bedroom. She picked it up and frowned at the blocked number. What potential clients would be calling this early on a Saturday morning?

"Hello?"

"Jaime Hensen?" The deep male voice with a Kentucky drawl sounded cautious.

"Speaking."

"Hi, this is Chief Petty Officer Stanton. I met you at Chris and Ma—Todd Hunter's wedding a while back."

Jaime searched through her memories. There'd been a lot of Navy guys at Chris's wedding, but she remembered that drawl like a favorite song. The hot, intense, and quiet member of Chris's SEAL team. *And the one I didn't go home with, dammit.*

"Oh, yes, Chief. I remember you. What can I do for

you?"

"I understand you're a private investigator specializing in missing persons, is that correct?"

"Yes, it is." That was disappointing. She'd hoped if the handsome chief ever called her, it would be for a date. "Do you know someone who's missing?"

"Yes, ma'am." The way he said it made her feel like he respected her as an expert, a rare thing from the men who became SEALs. "Can we meet for coffee to discuss it? It's kinda personal."

"Of course. I'd be happy to meet with you." Sure she'd prefer coffee with the prospect of sex, but a new job to take her mind off the anniversary of her sister's disappearance was good. *You need to make money, too.* "When and where?"

"The Island Breeze Café in thirty-five mikes?"

It took her a moment to translate 'mikes' into minutes. "Sounds good. I'll meet you there."

"Roger that. Er, sorry. See you soon, Ms. Hensen." He clicked off and she sighed. That sounded official. She'd rather be seeing him for a date, but at least she'd get to see him again.

Take what you can get, Hensen.

She surveyed her closet. Just because this was an official call didn't mean she couldn't look good. She chose a V-necked lavender top over black jeans and pulled her hair back into a loose French braid. Some tendrils snuck out past her ears, but she decided she liked the effect. She threw her windbreaker over her shoulders and added some lip gloss before heading out the door.

It didn't take long to reach the Island Breeze Café, but the wind had ramped up across the bay. She arrived more wind-blown than she intended, her carefully designed shabby-chic style reduced to flying wisps of auburn along her face. *So much for the professional look.* She tucked a few strands behind her ears and looked for Stanton.

She located him at a corner table with excellent access and vantage points over the exits. He sipped a cup of coffee, at apparent ease, but his gaze never stopped moving around the patrons of the café. *Definitely a sniper.*

Jaime didn't wave, suspecting he'd rather she didn't bring attention to his position. She wove through the tables to his and only held out her hand when she got close.

"Chief Stanton, good to see you again."

He rose and shook her hand. "And you, Ms. Hensen. Thanks for meetin' with me."

She loved his sweet Southern accent. It lent an old fashioned charm to the hard, calculating gaze scanning his surroundings. Not that he didn't focus on her, but she got the impression he still surveilled the people in the café. Though dressed casually in a long-sleeved t-shirt and faded jeans, he was every inch a soldier. She settled into the chair he pulled out for her and he joined her across the table.

"Not a problem. What can I do for you?"

He didn't answer for several breaths, but she couldn't read his expression at all to determine why. *Either he's reaffirming my identity, deciding how to kill me and hide the body, or mentally tallying the silverware supplied to each table.* She shivered, uncomfortable to be under the scrutiny of a man like Stanton, but she kept her expression open and polite. *What would it be like to see passion in those remote green eyes?* She ignored the accompanying thrill zinging through her.

"There's a person in my family who's missin' and no one has had any luck in finding her." Stanton's voice never fluctuated. He said it straight out, almost dead-pan, but his shoulders bunched and his jaw clenched in anger.

Jaime had become a master of microexpressions after she watched a popular TV show featuring the ability to read people. She'd taken classes in psychology, body language, and facial expressions to expand on the glossed-over version from the show. It fascinated her all the ways the body communicated without the use of the voice, even when someone was trying to hide something. The training had helped in her line of work, especially with missing persons cold cases. Relatives and friends often knew more than they said, and their bodies spoke volumes.

Jaime nodded and pulled out a notebook from her purse. Stanton tilted his head and a little smile curled his lips. *That's not sexy. Down, girl!*

"No Blackberry or tablet?"

"In this age of computer hackers and autocorrect, I prefer to write things down. Not only is it harder to copy, but I remember things better when I've written them myself. So." She set her purse on the empty chair beside her and raised her gaze to him expectantly. "Why don't you start at the beginning of who, when, where, why, what, and how, and we'll go from there."

Stanton leaned forward with his elbows on the table, a sigh deflating his chest. *And what a marvelous chest it is.* The corners of his mouth turned down, just for a second. *Guilt? Interesting.*

"Fifteen months ago in September, my younger sister went missing while out riding on our father's estate."

Their father's, but not theirs.

"What's your sister's name and how old is she?"

"Bethany Stanton and she would've turned thirty-one this March."

Jaime nodded. *Would've. He's already written her off.* "You said she was riding. Horse? Quad? Motorcycle? Bike?"

"Horse. Champion Quarter horse stallion. Her pride and joy."

And not cheap.

"We recovered the horse, but there was no sign of Bethany, nor of any struggle suggesting someone kidnapped her." His voice hardened as anger seeped in. "After three days, our father brought in a unit of Army

Special Forces to find her." Disgust radiated from his wrinkled nose and the corners of his mouth pulled down.

Jaime raised her eyebrows. "Army special forces? Not the FBI?"

Stanton sat back in his chair and licked the inside of his lower lip as he chose his words. She wondered how much of this was actually classified and could get her killed from just knowing. *Come on, Hensen, this isn't a spy flick.*

"My father is former senator William Stanton of Kentucky and was on several committees dealing with the security and protection of this country. He had many groups for use at his disposal." The chief shrugged. "He called in a unit called…" She swore he almost rolled his eyes. "SNAIFU."

Jaime blinked. "Snay-fu?"

"Supernatural Anomalies Investigative Field Unit."

She swallowed a laugh. "That's, uh, quite a mouthful." She wrote it down along with its acronym. "This unit really exists? It's not just something you're making up to get a date with me?"

Stanton cracked a half smile that curled Jaime's toes. "While I did want to see you again, Ms. Hensen, I'm not makin' this up. You won't find SNAIFU in the usual ways, but I know it's a real unit. The public has been kept in the dark about it because of their missions."

"The supernatural."

"Yeah."

Jaime couldn't hold back her laugh. "Come on. Vampires, werewolves, little green men, Area 51. Are you saying it's all real?"

"No, I'm sayin' there's a unit specifically charged with investigatin' supernatural anomalies, and they were the ones sent in to find my sister."

She shrugged. "Okay. And they've had no luck?"

"No. Worse, two members of the squad sent went missin' as well."

Jaime raised an eyebrow. "How do you know this? Were you there?"

Stanton shook his head. "No, I've been here in Coronado with my squad. At the time of Bethany's disappearance I was on a mission. But I still have friends in the grounds keepers and the stables of the estate and they told me what happened."

Jaime wrote notes. "Do you have any names of the soldiers who went missing? Or of their commanding officer? Maybe I can get some other information about Bethany from them."

Stanton frowned. "Here's the thing. The commanding officer was one of the ones gone missin'. I think his name was McMacken. That's what the stablehand said. One of the missin' did come back. A woman named Bryant, but she was whisked away pretty damn quick for debriefin'. I don't know any of the other names."

"What were they there to do other than find your sister?" When the Chief raised his eyebrows, she shrugged. "There had to be something going on because what was so supernatural about one young woman going missing? Obviously there was some reason to bring in SNAIFU."

Stanton lapsed into an intense, thoughtful silence, and Jaime tried to ignore how sexy it made him. He put all his energies into whatever he did and when it came to thinking, the intensity ramped up. *God, why didn't I go home with him after Chris's wedding?* He abruptly raised his gaze and swung it around the café as if looking for those who might be listening in. The hair on her arms rose in visceral awareness and she resisted the urge to smooth them down.

"How 'bout we take a walk along the pier? It's pretty nice today." He rose and shoved his arms into his leather jacket. He stood by her chair, waiting for her to comply.

It wasn't nice out. It was windy as hell with a winter bite in the air, but something about his secretiveness made her curious. What did he not want others to hear? She stood and followed him out into the windy morning. Fortunately, the sun took some of the chill out of the day and the enthusiasm of the college kids still on winter break was catching. In the sun, the ships moored at the pier carried a majesty she never tired of, and she let the small joys of the day lift some of her tension. But none of her curiosity.

Stanton led her to a bench set along the boardwalk under the shadows of some coconut palms, facing the moored battleships. He settled onto it, crossed his legs, and reclined at apparent ease with everything. But Jaime didn't buy it. He'd shaded his eyes with dark sunglasses, but she suspected he still scanned everywhere for listeners.

Jaime was determined to wait for a sign they'd arrived at some aural safe haven and sat down beside him, closing her eyes and inhaling the salty air. The wind blew her hair around, but she'd given up caring. At this point, her hair was the least of her concerns.

"The SNAIFU was brought in because there was somethin' weird happenin' on the grounds of the estate."

Stanton's voice sounded casual, like they were discussing the dimensions of the ships in front of them, but his words set her heart to fluttering. *Weird?*

"Was?"

"Yeah, things cleared up after the missing soldier came back."

Jaime shot him a flat look. "That's kinda convenient, isn't it?"

Stanton gave a one shouldered shrug. "Not really. None of the staff knew what was goin' on, but the members of SNAIFU have disappeared and Bethany's still missin'. And whatever brought the unit to the estate is gone. I'd say that's damn inconvenient."

Jaime heaved a sigh. "I don't know if I can help you. If something supernatural happened to your sister, I'm not sure I'll be any help in finding her. I don't do magic or X-Files stuff. I can find most people in *this* world. But if there's something else going on, I got nothin'."

For just a moment, Stanton's expression resembled William Wallace's when he discovered Robert the Bruce was on the side of Edward the Longshanks in the movie *Braveheart*. But his jaw hardened and his shoulders squared as he sat forward, bracing his elbows on his knees. "So you won't help me?"

"I didn't say that, Chief." Jaime tried to push aside the feeling she'd already let this man down. "Assuming for a moment your sister really did go somewhere beyond this world, and that's a huge assumption, I don't have any contacts who'd know anything about that. You'd probably have better luck trying to contact the SNAIFU."

He snorted in derision and she nodded. "Yeah, snowball's chance in hell. I get that."

A rueful smile quirked his lips and part of her danced an inner jig. *I made him smile!*

"But if there's a chance she came back like the missing soldier did, and she currently resides somewhere in this country or world, I can probably find her." She blinked and shook her head. "This sounds so crazy. Hypothetically speaking, do you really think there's something out of *Harry Potter* going on here?"

Stanton rubbed the back of his neck with one hand. "That's the thing, Ms. Hensen. I deal with facts and intel and provable events. But I've been a Special Warfare operator for a long time and I've seen stuff I didn't think existed before I saw it. Not dragons or unicorns or anythin' like that, but weird...stuff. If there is anythin' *Harry Potter* goin' on, Bethany's screwed. But I gotta believe she's somewhere here in our world. The powers-that-be just haven't looked hard enough." He lifted his glasses and met her gaze earnestly. "I need someone who can think outside the box, be smarter than the average bear, to find my sister. Do you think you can do that, Ms. Hensen?"

Jaime bit her tongue before she blurted anything

stupid. *Think. You can't promise him success no matter how sexy he is.* But she wanted to. She wanted to give him hope that success was no more than an in-depth search away.

"Tell you what, Chief. We'll go on the premise that she's here, in our world, and the magic and mythical have no play in this." *Are you listening to yourself? You're insane.* "I'll do what I can and chase down any leads or avenues I can find. And I'll keep you updated on any progress I make."

He nodded and she held up one finger. "But I need your word you'll let me know anything you find that might help. I understand you know secrets I can't know as a civilian, but anything you find out about your sister or the SNAIFU would help my efforts. Deal?"

Stanton held out his hand. "Deal, Ms. Hensen. How much do you charge for your services?"

"Usually, I charge ten grand and you get three months of in-depth research and effort of my time."

His face turned to solid marble for all it moved. She suspected she was a bit rich for his blood.

"But since you're in the active military, I'll give you a discount of forty percent off my usual expenses." She tipped her head. "You'll still get at least three months of my time and efforts, but on a portion of the cost."

He stared at her a long time without saying anything and she wondered what he thought of both her normal costs and the discount. She didn't want to insult him either way, but this was her business and her career. She was damn good at what she did and worth the expenses. And some part of her wanted him to be impressed with her efforts.

"Will you be taking other jobs during that time?"

"If something comes up." She shrugged. "But as of right now I'm between jobs."

"So you'll have no other income than what I pay you."

She shrugged again. "Yes, that's right."

Stanton dropped his chin to his chest and his jaw tightened. "Tell you what. Why don't I pay you thirty-five hundred a month for each month you search for Bethany. That way you get paid your normal fees for the work, and I still can afford groceries."

So, not a trust-fund baby. Jaime tilted her head. "Are you sure? You're active military and I know the pay isn't astronomical."

"You're right, it's not, but I'm sure. This is important. Family is important." He heaved a big sigh that made his broad shoulders stretch his t-shirt and her nipples hardened at the thought of those lovely muscles. "Bethany's really all the family I have."

"What about your father, Senator Stanton?"

The chief shook his head. "He lost his last bid for reelection when my sister went missin', and he wrote me off years ago when I became a SEAL. I suspect both of us are disappointments to him, but considerin' what a womanizin' asshole he is, it's not that big o'deal."

"But you said it yourself. Family is important."

Stanton snorted. "He's not family. He's just a sperm donor."

Damn, I guess the Beatles were right. Money can't buy love. Her family hadn't had much financially, especially after her sister's disappearance, but Jaime and her mother had bonded until the cancer ended mom's life.

"Ouch. Remind me not to go to your family reunions."

He snorted. "Remind *me* not to go, either." He sighed again. "So, will you take the job and try to find Bethany for me?"

Jaime nodded and held out her hand. "Yes, sir. I'm happy to take the job. If you'll follow me back to my office, we'll put it in writing so we both know what's what."

He took her hand and the heat of his palm flooded up her arm and into her chest. Her nipples hardened again and she resisted the urge to drag him close enough to rub them against him. Instead, she cautioned herself to simply shake his hand firmly and prepared to let go. *This isn't a romantic date, it's a business transaction.*

But Stanton wouldn't let go and he stared at her from behind his dark glasses for several heartbeats. Her snarky side wanted to make a wise crack about needing her hands, but the horny side duct-taped the snark into the recesses of her mind.

"I know we have business to discuss, or at least put in ink, but I really regret not contactin' you after the weddin' when I had leave." He gave a one shoulder shrug. "How 'bout I treat you to breakfast? After all, I dragged you out early to talk about business on a Saturday. What do you say?"

Jaime blinked. *He wants a date? Yeah, baby.* She tried to think of her schedule for the day, but her mind kept blanking each time his arm flexed in his tight shirt. *I don't really have any plans for today beyond going to the gym.*

"Yeah, all right. Breakfast sounds great." He finally let her hand go and she missed the warm roughness of his palm.

"Good. Let's go back to the Island Breeze. They have the best huevos rancheros in Coronado." He rose and held his hand out to her and she didn't hesitate to take it.

Hell no, I'll take every chance to touch him.

He tucked her hand into the crook of his elbow and she curled her fingers around his hard leather-covered forearm. She loved the old-world charm to his actions, yet it didn't feel like he saw her as less than capable.

"How did you find out what I did for a living, Chief?"

Stanton shrugged. "I could say somethin' real smug like I did research, but really it was Chris Hunter who told me to call you."

Jaime laughed. "Thanks for being honest."

"Yeah, sometimes it's the best policy." He flashed a

grin. "Chris said you specialized in missin' people and that's what convinced me."

She shot him a rueful smile. "So it wasn't my good looks or charm that did it?"

"Aw hell, Ms. Hensen, it was just a bonus. I woulda called you eventually, but this just killed two birds with one stone." He pushed open the doors of the Island Breeze Café and gestured for her to pick a table.

"Nothing like stoned birds to make a woman's day."

He laughed and she grinned as she slid into a booth. "Let me order somethin' to drink before it gets too crazy in here. What would you like?"

"Some coffee would be nice. I haven't had any yet this morning."

"Yeah, I'm sorry about that, but hopefully this'll make up for it."

She watched him saunter to the front counter to sweet-talk the waitress and enjoyed his ass in his form-fitting jeans. *Hell yeah, he definitely makes up for missing coffee first thing.*

Now if she could only see his ass without the jeans. *You might have to keep him locked up in your room at that point.* Yeah, like that would ever happen. Not only were they just business acquaintances, but he was a frickin' U.S. Navy SEAL. SEALs didn't stay locked up anywhere.

A shiver of excitement rippled through her. Something about the SEALs' nearly inhuman ability to do anything turned her on. *Including die.* Yeah, that was the problem. Each time he went out on a mission he might not come back. She shoved the thought away as Chief Stanton returned to the table with a sultry smile and two cups of black coffee.

"I didn't know if you took it light and sweet or black, so I figured I'd let you doctor it yourself." He paused and tilted his head. "Everythin' okay? You looked kinda grim there for a moment."

So much from hiding her thoughts from a sniper, a man trained to see things most ignored.

Jaime shook her head. "Just letting my mind run away from me, and as usual, jumping the gun."

He smiled again as he sat down. "Good thing I know my weapons. I got lots of "guns" to jump."

She laughed. "Without a doubt." Like a shadow fleeing the sun, the darkness of her thoughts dissipated and she grabbed some packages of creamer. "If you want to know, I take my coffee light, but not sweetened."

"Duly noted, ma'am."

"Jaime."

"Beg your pardon?"

She'd love it if he begged her for something, but she'd settle for repeating what she'd said. "You can call me Jaime since you're taking me to breakfast, and we almost hooked up at the wedding."

"Jaime." He rolled the sound over his tongue and she swore her temperature rose. "Pretty name. Strong, capable, and resourceful."

"Thanks. It means 'I love' in French because my mom was such a romantic. I always thought it sounded like 'James.'"

"So what do you love, Jaime?" He sipped his coffee as the edges of his mouth curled.

"I'd love to know your first name so I don't just call you by your rank." She raised an eyebrow.

He grinned. "What if my first name is Chief?"

"You mean like in *Catch 22* where the character is known as Major Major Major Major?"

He laughed. "A woman who knows classic literature. Hooyah. My given name is Kevin Wickham Stanton, but my friends call me Rimshot."

"Rimshot? Because you're a sniper?"

He nodded. "Because while in sniper school I managed to wing the target a few times before finding my center.

The nickname stuck."

"Rimshot." She liked the name even if he inherited it for a mistake. "Who gets to call you Kevin?"

He picked up the menu and pretended to scan the contents. "My mother and sister."

"You know it's from the Old Irish meaning 'kind, gentle, and handsome.'" She tilted her head and smiled. "So far I think it fits."

"Oh yeah?" He laughed and it lit more excitement inside her. "Two out of three ain't bad. Not sure how handsome I am."

"You don't have to be sure. I am." And she winked.

CHAPTER THREE

A grin stretched across his face. "Yes, ma'am."

Damn, this woman had sass and could easily stroke his ego without much effort. *I'd let her stroke more than that.* When she'd first walked into the café this morning his cock hardened the moment he caught sight of her glorious wavy, auburn hair. With her curves encased in cotton and soft denim, he'd itched to run his hands over them, but he'd reined in his libido in favor of business.

Now, he could enjoy the flirting and conversation. Back at the wedding, she'd surprised him with being more than the typical Navy bunnies, women looking for some hot SEAL cock. Jaime had personality and intelligence as well as a great ass. He liked her forthrightness and her knowledge of classic literature. Contrary to popular belief about SEALs, he liked to read some of those epic novels when he had time between missions. *Catch 22* had been one of the more mind-bending tales.

He gestured to the menus. "Should we order breakfast? Just talkin' to you makes me work up an appetite."

"Oh, yes. I'm starved."

Thank the good Lord she didn't look it. He preferred his women curvy and soft, yet fit and strong. Jaime didn't look like she could run a marathon, but the padding on her body settled on her boobs and butt, just where he liked it.

"We can't have that. Let's order before you wilt."

"Heh. No chance of that. I've never swooned in my life."

"Oh yeah?" He'd like her to swoon over him. "Why's that?"

She dipped her chin, shooting him a look from under her brows. "No one was ever there to catch me. I've been my own hero for a long time."

I'd change that in a heartbeat, sweetheart. "Maybe you ain't found the right man for the job."

"Oh, that's definitely true." She shook her head and smiled. "But I found I prefer to save my own ass rather than wait on him."

"Ouch." He pressed his fist to his chest over his heart. "Even heroes need at team behind them. What happened to your team?"

To his surprise, the humor left her face. "After my sister disappeared, my family kinda fell apart and the 'all for one, one for all' went by the wayside."

His gut tightened at the sorrow in her voice, but the waitress came over to take their orders and he had to hold his questions. Jaime smiled and made her selection, but the smile didn't return to her eyes and Kevin kicked himself for killing her mood. The waitress took their choices and he wondered if Jaime would talk more about her family.

"Is that why you became a private investigator specializing in missing persons?"

She shot him a confused look before her mind caught up on the conversation. "Oh, yes."

"What happened?"

Jaime sighed and sipped some of her coffee. "I don't really know. My sister was in high school, four years older than me. Near as I can find out, she'd gone out clubbing with her friends and these college guys they'd met.

Everyone was drinking and dancing." She shrugged and he filled in the blanks. *Everyone drunk and not paying attention.*

"She went to the bathroom and never came back. No one noticed until they got ready to leave." A horrible grimace pulled Jaime's lips down. "She'd left her purse and cell phone on the table, so no way to track her. And this was back when cell phones were a new thing."

"Didn't the cops do anythin'?"

"What could they do? The club didn't have cameras in the bathrooms and there were too many people in the club that night. No one had seen her leave and her friends couldn't remember when she'd left the table." Jaime shook her head. "I've been over all the evidence of that night and leading up to it. All the leads hit a dead end."

"I'm sorry, Jaime." He understood the feeling of futility, of not even knowing which way to turn. It didn't happen often in the Teams, but he'd experienced it with regards to Bethany. *At least I have Jaime to help me.* She hadn't had anyone. *No wonder she always saves herself now.*

"Thanks. I haven't given up looking. I owe it to Mia."

"How long has it been?"

"Just over twenty-two years."

Holy shit!

She shrugged, reading his exclamation in his widened eyes. "Yeah, I've heard all the reasons to give up. The likelihood of her being alive is slim-to-none and Slim went home, but I owe it to her and my family to find her body if that's all there is left. In the meantime, I can help other families recover their loved ones so they don't have to go through the same heartache. Like your family."

"Yeah, well, if you do this for me, you'll be helping all the family Bethany has."

Jaime blinked, but said nothing as the waitress came with their orders. She shot a distracted smile at the server when she suggested they enjoy their meals, but her gaze returned to his face as soon as the woman stepped away.

"What about your parents?"

Kevin shrugged. "My mama died in a car crash almost ten years ago now, and our grandparents died a few years before that."

"And your father's just a sperm donor?"

Anger rose so swiftly, he slammed his Samurai Mask into place before it showed on his face. He took a few deep breaths and focused on his food for a short time as he beat the anger into submission.

"Daddy had more interest in money, politics, and power then he ever did in family. When he lost the last election and the money set aside for Bethany by our Granddad, he lost interest in putting more effort or money into finding her."

Jaime's eyes widened. "Are you serious?"

"Yes, ma'am." He stuffed some pancake in his mouth to keep from snarling. Bethany meant the world to him, the only family who understood his need to be a SEAL.

"Damn, I'm sorry, Kevin." Jaime reached across and laid her hand on his forearm. "I'll do my best and we'll find her. I promise."

He nodded. "Thanks, Jaime. But I'm pretty sure you can't promise that."

"Yes, I can. I have a gut feeling about this one."

"You have that same gut feeling about your own sister?"

Jaime drew back as if he'd slapped her and he inwardly cursed. *Don't take your anger at your father out on her, jackass.* "I'm sorry, Jaime. That was a low blow and came from the anger at my father for doin' nothin'."

She cleared her throat and chopped up her sausage with more force than necessary for a few moments. Emotions flashed across her face and her jaw tightened, but she took her time before she answered him in a calm voice.

"As it happens, yes, I had a gut feeling about my sister and it hasn't waned despite twenty-two years. Every clue I find brings me a step closer and fans the feeling." She met his gaze with challenge in her golden brown eyes. "But if you'd like to wallow in doubt and self-pity, you're more than welcome to do so. I thought SEALs always saw the possibilities, but I've only really known Chris well. I'll just keep my optimism to myself, then."

Damn, the woman had a tongue like a whip and he felt the blow as much as when he'd lashed out at her. *And I deserve every stroke.* Anger and disgust tightened her shoulders as she lapsed into an icy silence. He wanted to punch himself in the gut, but in lieu of that, he dredged his courage out of the trash bin and reached across the table to touch the back of her hand with one finger.

"I'm truly sorry, Jaime. It was rude and uncalled for. Please, accept my apologies. Can we start over?"

"How would you like to start over, Chief?" She met his gaze and all the friendliness had disappeared from her expression. "Do you even want me to look into your sister's disappearance? You seem convinced it's a lost cause. We haven't signed a contract or exchanged money yet. You can always back out now."

"No, ma'am, I don't wanna do that." What did Magic do when he needed to calm folks down? *Use the accent.* "I'm real sorry, Ms. Hensen. Please forgive me and don't give up on Bethany. I do need your help and I need you on my team. If there's one thing SEALs know well, it's how important our Team is."

He held her gaze and forced himself to show her his contrition. He wasn't very good at it, but he'd screwed up and he knew it. *Please God don't let her turn me down.* He didn't pray or beg often, but he figured after such a shitty year he'd earned a little grace.

Jaime chewed her food and swallowed before she said a word. She gave nothing away as she took a sip of coffee to wash the rest down and set her cup rather precisely beside her plate.

"All right, Chief. Here's how this is gonna go. We're gonna make this deal and sign a contract. If at any time you decide it's not going anywhere or I'm not all I say I am and you wanna quit, let me know and I'll prorate my fees up to that point. We got a deal, SEAL?"

Kevin had a déjà vu moment where he swore he heard his BUD/S instructor roaring at him, *You tired? You wanna quit? The bell's right over there, Stanton. Ring out and go home!* He gritted his teeth against the returning snarl and nodded.

"Yes, ma'am, we got a deal. And for the record, I'm sorry I was such an unmitigated jackass. My mama taught me better than that and I'll take any butt-whoopin' you feel necessary to dish out."

Jaime snorted. "I thought SEALs dealt in ass-kickings."

"Yes, ma'am, we do, but it just depends on which part of the country you hail from. In Kentucky, we get butt-whoopin's."

A half smile curled her lips. "We could compromise with an ass-whoopin' and bring the two sides of the country together."

"That'd be just fine." He held out his hand to her. "You've got yourself a deal."

She grasped his palm and the rightness of holding hers ricocheted through his awareness. *This woman is my destiny.* The thought surprised him so much he almost let go, but like all the trials in BUD/S, he stuck it out, determined to see it through. His mother once told him her family had the gift of foresight, some stronger than others. He'd thought she might be pulling his leg since she'd ended up with his bastard of a father, but holding Jaime's hand brought awareness to how right it felt.

"Good." She pulled away and he reluctantly let her go.

"Then once we're done with breakfast, I'll head over to my office and work up the contract so we both know where we stand."

The last thing he wanted was to let her go, but being clingy this early in their relationship would send up a warning flare. *And it is a relationship, or will be soon.* Even if they didn't find Bethany, he wanted more time with Jaime Hensen. But he believed in her.

Two birds with one stone.

"Sounds like a plan. Let me give you my cell number so if you find anything you can call or text me." He pulled out his phone and she raised an eyebrow.

"You can't remember?"

He laughed. "No, I thought I'd text it to you. I keep personal info like that close to my chest." *Right where I'd like to keep you.*

"Oh, yeah, of course."

"There." He hit send. "Now you can get a hold of me anytime you need me."

"Anytime?" She added a smile to her raised eyebrow. "A SEAL?"

"Touché."

They finished their breakfasts and he paid the check while she wrote some notes into her notebook. The moment where he'd have to let her go approached and his gut clenched. He wanted more time. *Dammit, I'll make time.* He had leave unless his CO called him to go wheels-up, and he'd use all of it to hang with Jaime if she'd let him.

"So, what are you doin' tonight?"

"Tonight?" She blinked as she set her phone in her purse. "Uh, well, I hadn't planned anything other than doing some preliminary work on your sister's case. Why?"

"How about we have a working dinner together?"

She raised both eyebrows this time. "You want to have dinner with me, too? Moving kinda fast, aren't you?"

His gut clenched at the idea she'd turn him down, but

he shrugged. "Hey, I'm a SEAL. We don't get much time between missions and I gotta make my moves when I can." He sobered and gave her an earnest stare. "I like you, Jaime, and want more time with you. SEALs don't get a lot of guarantees. Well other than visiting hot zones, and I don't want to let this opportunity slip through my fingers. So if you're willin', I'd like to spend more time with you tonight."

A slow smile slid across her lips. "All right, Chief. Tell you what. I'll get my initial assessment on your sister's case done along with the contract then meet you at my office around six for dinner. Sound good?"

"Sounds great, and the name's Kevin." He stood with her as she rose, only half surprised he'd insisted on her using his given name. "Gotta maintain my reputation as kind, gentle, and handsome."

Jaime laughed as she threw her purse over her shoulder. "Right. Okay, Kevin. See you at my office at six."

They left the café and he escorted her to her car. "Where's your office located?"

"You're a big, bad Navy SEAL. Do a little recon and figure it out. See you tonight."

She winked and slid into her front seat. Kevin laughed, enchanted by both the woman and the challenge as she drove away. *Damn.*

****

Rimshot drove back to base and headed for the gym to distract himself from the alluring memories of Jaime's hair shining in the sunshine of the wharf. Despite the punishing workout, his mind still focused on the sway of her hips as she'd walked away and the way her top molded around her breasts.

Fuck!

Working out with a hard-on wasn't comfortable, but having one while in the shower was bound to get comments and looks. *Think about PT or missing a target.* That usually brought his cock to heel, and it certainly helped this time. By the time he'd finished and headed for the shower, his body had returned to normal.

Deli must have finished in the gym about the same time because the shorter man stood in front of his locker when Kevin came out of the showers.

"Hey, Deli. How's it goin'?"

"Good." His squad mate nodded as he jerked his sweat-stained shirt over his head. Deli stood shorter than Kevin's sister Bethany, but the man carried himself with a confidence born of experience and skill. Bullet scars marked his back in a few places where he'd earned his stripes.

"Can you believe Bronco's gonna be a dad?" Kevin rubbed a towel over his head.

Deli shook his head. "It's a helluva thing. No way in hell I'm ready for that shit."

"Roger that."

"Hey, if you're not doin' nothin' later, maybe we can go for a beer at the Surf 'N Turf."

"Yeah, sure. I got time right now. Why don't we do lunch?"

"Give me ten to shower and I'll meet you outside." Deli headed for the showers.

"Roger that." Kevin zipped up his gym bag and ambled out of the locker room. He liked Deli for all the guy tended to be chatty. *Good thing because I don't talk much.* The shorter man often filled in the long silences. Kevin leaned against a concrete retaining wall beneath a palm tree to wait.

Less than ten minutes later, Deli sauntered out of the gym dressed in a GO NAVY t-shirt and sweatpants. The guy might be short, but his personality could fill a room.

Before he'd become a SEAL he would've been a candidate for "punk with little-man complex", but now the confidence and experience translated without the overt displays of ego.

"Your wheels or mine?" Deli also loved his new Jeep Patriot. *Small yet tough, like him.*

"Yours are fine." Kevin didn't mind letting Deli drive. His Patriot still had the "new car" smell every guy loved.

"Wicked."

He followed Deli to the shiny navy blue Jeep and slid into the hot interior. They had to roll down the windows to breathe, but once they got moving, the air cooled.

"It's a nice ride, Deli." Kevin leaned his elbow on the door.

"Thanks. It's a pretty good chick-magnet."

Kevin laughed and they chatted about nothing while the shorter SEAL drove to the bar. The tourists had increased despite the cooler temperatures and they had to dodge some of the MLK-weekend crowd trying to get into the restaurants for lunch specials. Kevin found them a quiet table at the Surf 'N Turf and he ordered a burger along with his beer. Deli ordered a full sized pizza and Kevin didn't bother to ask if he wanted the leftovers. The man might have short stature, but he could pack away more food than the rest of them.

Kevin tucked into his burger and fries when they arrived, his mind homing back to his missing sister. Bethany never strayed far his thoughts, especially now with Jaime's involvement. Usually, the thought of Bethany's disappearance made his gut ache, but now a slow smile curled his lips. If Jaime succeeded, he'd get to both spend more time with her and see his sister again.

"Hey, what's the grin for, Rimshot?"

Kevin blinked as the bar and his table companion came back into focus. "What?"

"You're grinning like the Cheshire Cat at your food.

Something extra tasty?"

"Nah, it's fine. Just thinkin' about my sister."

"Thinkin' about your sister makes you grin?"

Kevin gave a one-shouldered shrug.

"Or is it that sexy red-head Chris told you to call?"

Kevin had to slip on the Samurai Mask to keep from blushing. "Could be."

Deli laughed. "Thought so. So will she take the case?"

"Yeah, I called her. We're meetin' later to sign the contract and get details ironed out."

"That's good, right? I mean, she's a professional and all."

Yeah, it was good, if Jaime could actually do anything. But if the U.S. Army with their special SNAIFU squad couldn't do it, he didn't have a lot of hope for a civilian. *Don't knock it till you try it.* He knew better than to voice his doubts, though. Jaime would walk and then no one would help him find Bethany.

"Yeah, she's professional. I'm givin' it a chance. If it don't work, I'll be no worse off." Kevin nodded. "Better'n the old man. He's not doin' a damn thing about it, even when Bethany disappeared right off his estate."

"Damn, that's messed up. Sounds like your family needs better security." Deli swallowed the bite of pizza he had in his mouth and grimaced. "Damn west coast. Can't make a decent pie even when you pay 'em."

Deli's complaint made Kevin chuckle. "Yeah, well the next time you have time, you can school 'em, Deli."

"Eh, I don't have time. Heathens."

Kevin laughed. "I'm sure you could teach 'em to do it right."

Deli grumbled, but kept eating.

"You said you knew about a new security company last night at Bronco's party. What was all that about?"

"What, GAPS?" Deli took a swig of beer to wash down the pizza.

"Yeah. What does it stand for?"

"It's pretty slick. Guardian Angel Protection Services, precision security to fill in the GAPs in yours." Deli grinned. "We cover your six when God's too busy."

"Well hell, that is slick. How do you know so much about it?"

"I got a buddy who's part of the core crew. Rick Mann. You ever worked with him?"

"Nah, why would I?"

Deli shrugged. "I was on a joint op in Afghanistan and partnered with him before I came here to Beta Squad. We kept in touch after and that's how I found out about his new venture."

"He still active and doin' this at the same time?"

"Nah, he was medically retired here a while back."

Kevin grunted. "What kind of protection services do they offer?"

"Mostly large scale cargo and shipments from big companies in hot zones." Deli shrugged. "Or places that aren't considered hot but could get that way damn fast, especially without the right kind of operators. Most of these guys are retired SEALs."

Kevin grunted, his mind returning to his sister Bethany. "Think they do rescue and recovery missions?"

"I dunno, man. Sometimes they even do private security like for celebrities and weddings of bigwigs. But I get the impression they're looking for the big bucks, and given their skills, they deserve it. You'd at least have to get someone with deep pockets involved to interest them." Deli took a swig of his beer. "They're a security company, protecting cargo and shit like that. They're essentially mercs doing the same ops without waiting for Command's thumbs-up. Seems like a good place to end up after I retire."

"If they get paid the way you're talkin', hell yeah it would be good. Who wouldn't want a bunch of SEALs protecting your back?"

"Yeah. And most of these guys were DEVGRU, the best of us."

"Damn." Rimshot sighed. "Think they'd go after my sister? I mean, SEALs step up when needed for family."

Deli shook his head. "I don't think it's beyond their abilities, but not within the purview of their company. They make sure shit doesn't go missing the first time."

"Yeah. Sure wish my daddy thought to have them around when Bethany went missin'. Of course, why the hell would he need anyone on his own estate?" He crumpled up his paper napkin and tossed it in the empty food basket. "It's fucked up six ways from breakfast."

"Damn. I'm sorry, Rimshot." Deli scowled.

Kevin ran a hand over his face, thinking he'd need to shave before he saw Jaime that night. The smile almost cracked his lips again, but the thought of Bethany sobered him. "She's missin' and I'm trained for shit like this, but I can't do a damn thing about it."

"Yeah, but at least you have someone willing to make an effort. That's something." Deli tucked into another slice. "Plus, she's hot and smart."

"How d'you know that?"

Deli snorted. "I was at the wedding too, dumbass. Not only could she hold a conversation, she looked amazing in that dress and could dance your ass off. Like I said, hot."

Kevin said nothing, but wondered if he'd have to hide Jaime from the rest of the squad until he'd secured her affections. *'Cause, she's mine and I ain't sharin'.* He stuffed the rest of his burger into his mouth to keep from saying anything stupid or possessive. *But she sure is gonna be mine.*

CHAPTER FOUR

Jaime hit the ground running as soon as she got back to her office and fired up the computer search engines. She also opened up a standard contract for the Chief to sign for her services. She didn't like to have to charge him the full amount. *The military deserves a discount, right?* But he'd insisted and she didn't want to insult him by suggesting he couldn't afford her. *Ugh, more-than-business relationships are complicated.*

She filled out the contract and saved it as the web pages and search sources loaded up. She'd long had contacts with the National Missing Persons Database, which stored details like finger prints, dental records, blood type, and brief family history on anyone who'd been reported missing for the last twenty years. Older records were slowly being updated and added to the registry, and it remained fairly up to date. Her current case was only chilled, not gravestone-cold. *Like Mia's.* Jaime's files on her sister's disappearance were distressingly thick, but even with all the info she'd gathered, it still wasn't enough to find her.

Bethany Stanton's information came up immediately. Five foot eight inches in height, thirty years of age, a hundred and thirty-nine pounds, blonde, hazel eyes, and the daughter of former Kentucky senator William Stanton. She'd disappeared off her father's estate a little more than a year ago. No sign of struggle, no strangers on the grounds at the time of her disappearance, no threats or ransom notes received.

A picture of a pretty woman sharing Kevin's nose and chin sat beside the description and Jaime clicked on it to enlarge the image. She stood beside a chestnut horse with a white blaze down its face. The caption read, "Bethany Stanton with champion Quarter Horse, Killian Ford's Tenpenny."

Maybe it has something to do with the horse.

She opened up the local newspaper and national news sources to search for Bethany or Killian Ford's Tenpenny, and found information on both the woman's disappearance and the wins she accrued with the chestnut quarter horse.

Later articles reported on the recovery of the horse despite Ms. Stanton's disappearance, and finally the sale of Killian for $2.5 million to a breeder somewhere in California. Jaime frowned. From all accounts, the horse was Ms. Stanton's favorite. *Her pride and joy, Kevin said.* Why would the Stanton family sell the animal?

Kevin's sneer filled Jaime's mind along with his hard words pertaining to his father. *A womanizing asshole.* Not exactly Father-of-the-year material.

"So did he sell the horse because he couldn't stand the reminder of her disappearance or because he wanted the money?"

Nothing in the articles gave Jaime that information, but in the long run it didn't matter. Bethany was gone, the horse had been sold, and the senator lost the election and his daughter. *And a partridge in a pear tree. Whee!*

Despite her sarcastic thoughts, her gut said to follow the horse. Something about it didn't sit right about the disposal of such an asset, but the trail went cold, at least on the surface. According to the records, the horse still resided with a Quarter Horse breeder in California named Whitewater Farms, but after more digging, no one matching Bethany's description worked for or around the stable. She did find out Whitewater Farms was owned by Ian and Tabitha McMacken, and their daughter, Tricia McMacken had disappeared over a decade earlier in Las Vegas.

Gone without a trace. No signs of struggle, no ransom note. Curiously coincidental. Jaime didn't believe in coincidences anymore than she believed in unicorns. But this family had been devastated and had put their monies into their horses and their business because as quoted, "Tricia loved them and that's all we have left of her." They had another child, a son, who'd joined the Army, but not much was said about him.

Wait a minute...

Jaime grabbed her notebook and flipped through the pages while talking with Stanton. She scanned her scrawled words and stopped when they talked about the SNAIFU. *Commanding officer named McMacken (sp?).* Jaime sat back in her chair and stared at the wall behind the monitor for a moment. *There can't be that many McMackens in the U.S. Army, can there?*

She pulled up the Army personnel database and found fifteen men with the last name McMacken in their records. Eight were dead, killed in every war from World War Two to Iraq and Afghanistan. Of the seven others still alive, only three could be considered commanding officers and one was a two star general. A wounded veteran held the rank of captain, and a major had been honorably discharged and dropped off the grid.

Well, hell.

Captain E. Roger McMacken recovered at the new VA hospital in Las Vegas. *At least he's in Vegas, baby.* Between him, the general Sean L. McMacken, and the discharged major Stephen P. McMacken, she didn't have a lot to go on, but maybe the captain and the general could at least account for their whereabouts at the time Bethany had disappeared. The major's service record had been sealed, but he'd grown up in California, and was related to Ian and Tabitha. They'd probably have an idea where he'd ended up.

But this is moot. Didn't the SNAIFU CO go missing?

Jaime sighed and wrote their names down anyway. *No stone left unturned.* She'd contact the owners of Whitewater Farms to find out if they had contact information for their son and to see if they had any interest in looking for their daughter. *Two birds with one stone, as Kevin would say.*

The reminder of the handsome SEAL made her smile and she reached for her phone to call her best friend Chris. As the first female Navy SEAL, Chris had won a place of honor in the annals of history, but she still kept a relatively low profile out of habit. Despite the internet's best efforts, SEALs served because most were heroic at heart. *And they want to blow shit up.* They didn't need accolades or huge banners flying in the sky for their accomplishments. They did what they did because it needed to be done, not for the recognition of having done it.

Jaime tapped her phone and held it to her ear, listening to the rings.

"The Hunters."

The voice on the other end held warning and understated threat. After Chris and the other SEALs' wives were abducted the year before, Chris had adopted the idea of making it very clear who all lived at her house. Hell, even her former squadmate Jim Waters moved in with them, bringing the badassary to the highest setting ever. *Not to mention the sexiness.*

"Hey, Chris, it's me."

"Hey Jaime. What's going on?" Humor and warmth

heated Chris's voice and the threat retreated into the background.

"Chief Stanton called me."

Chris laughed. "Rimshot? Good. I'm glad to hear that. Will you be able to help him?"

"Yeah, I think so. You know how these things go. Could take a week or two, could take years." Jaime shrugged even though her friend couldn't see it. "But that's not why I called. Why didn't you tell me he smelled so damn good?"

Chris laughed again. "Does he? Usually when I was with him, we all smelled so bad, either from sweat, dirt, or briny seawater that I never noticed."

"He definitely didn't smell like that today." No, he'd smelled like hot man and coffee, and those two things made up her favorite meals. "He also took me out to breakfast."

"Oh yeah?" Chris sounded amused. "It's about time."

"What's that supposed to mean?"

"Hey, I might have been getting married, but I saw how Stanton looked at you that day."

"A lot of guys 'looked at me' that day."

"Uh-huh, but Stanton *never* looks at women like that. The man is a glacier."

Jaime snorted. "A glacier?"

"Yep. Hard, cold, unmoving, and solid. Nothing ever fazes him."

"I don't think that's true." Not after how he took his frustration with his father out on her. "I think he's pretty upset about his sister going missing."

"Yeah, I know." Chris sighed. "But the good news is he called you for help. Big step for a SEAL, especially a sniper. He could use some good news. Magic and Retro, I mean, Todd and Jim say he's been more distant than usual."

"It wouldn't surprise me if he's worried about his sister. He's probably stuck in his head because he can't do a damn thing about her disappearance."

"So you're gonna take the job?"

"Yeah. And I'm going to find her, Chris. I got a gut feeling about it."

Stanton's snarky words came back to her, but she shoved them aside. Her gut had been right more times than not, and she'd learned to follow it over the years. Something about Bethany Stanton's horse Killian would pan out. She didn't know how yet, but she could wait for the clues to fall into place.

"Stick with that, even if Stanton gives you the side-eye." Chris's voice had grown serious. "I've known you long enough to remember all those times you found missing kids. Hell, I might have been in the SEALs, but I remember the big story Channel 12 did on you and your work exposing the China Town Kidnapping Ring in San Francisco."

Jaime nodded and grimaced. It had been a landmark case and gotten her the publicity to make her business take off. Wealthy, infertile parents, both domestically and internationally, paid good money to adopt children of Asian descent. The organization supplying the children had no qualms taking kids off the streets on their way home from school or daycare.

But when a Hollywood actress's kid went missing, one of Jaime's friends from high school in the actress's entourage mentioned her name and Jaime helped recover the child, as well as many more who'd been abducted. She'd worked with SFPD missing persons a few times after that, pooling their resources, especially for high-profile cases. She made a good living, but the China Town Kidnapping had really put her on the map.

"Yeah, but that was good, old fashioned detective work."

"Don't sideline your gut, Jaime. You told me back then you had a gut feeling about the case and look how that turned out."

"So what does it say that I've always had a gut feeling about my own sister's case?"

"That you just have to wait for the right time to act on it." Chris paused and Jaime could almost see her choosing her words. "Speaking of which, are there any changes in that?"

Jaime sighed. "No, nothing. But I've been keeping my ear to the ground and keeping track of any missing persons stories featuring young Caucasian women between the ages of eighteen and twenty-five to see if there are any similarities." She shivered. "It's caught a few serial killers along the way, but none of the bodies or skeletons matched my sister. But the gut feeling persists."

She'd also put out the word to some of her contacts in the various police departments with her sister's description, but nothing panned out so far. They all promised her they'd keep an eye out and pass along any information remotely associated with Mia's disappearance. She'd agreed to do the same for them.

"Trust it. It's saved me and Beta Squad more times than I can count."

"Yeah? Even if I've got nothing?"

"Even so. Let it sit there. Eventually it'll either give you a hint of the direction you need to look or something else will crop up just when you need it."

"Let's hope so." Jaime shrugged off her usual frustration over her sister. "But that's not why I'm calling. I wanted to let you know I'm going on a real date tonight with Chief Stanton...you know, just in case my body turns up."

Chris laughed. "Shut up, stop being so fucking morbid. I'd be more worried about you when out doing an investigation than I would with Rimshot."

"I know." Jaime grinned at the phone. "I just figured you should know there's a good likelihood he'll get laid tonight, so if you see him around and he's less glacial than usual, it's because I jumped his bones."

"I'll pass the word on to Todd and Jim. They'll probably do a couple of 'high fives' and then razz Rimshot about it."

"Hey, give me the 411 on this whole living-with-Jim thing. Why is he really there at your house, Chris?"

A long pause filled the air on the other side of the phone and Jaime wondered if she'd crossed a line with her friend. She and Chris had known each other since high school and traded dating horror stories, but once Chris entered the SEALs, she hadn't talked much about her love life. *If she even had one.* After her brush with death on her last mission with the SEALs, she'd talked to Jaime about her love for Todd "Magic" Hunter and Jim "Retro" Waters. She'd loved them equally, but settled on marrying Todd. Despite that, Jim had never been far and treated Chris as much like his wife as Todd's.

"I'm married to both of them, Jaime."

Jaime sat back in her chair, her mind going blank. "What?"

"Not according to the State of California, of course, but I'm married to Todd and Jim in every other way that counts." She paused again. "It's what we've always wanted and it works for us. I don't really expect anyone to understand, but I told myself I'd be honest with you if you ever asked. So, yeah."

Jaime turned over the information in her mind. "Two men? And not just any men, but two Navy SEALs? The Alphas of the alphas? Damn, lady, how the hell did you get so lucky?"

"So you're not freaked out or anything?" She'd never heard Chris sound so hesitant.

Jaime gave herself time to think. "No, I'm not freaked out. I'm not sure I could do it, but if it works for you and you're all happy, I'm good with it. How did you get the guys to agree? I mean I wouldn't expect SEALs to be sexually open to stuff like that, but maybe that's because I forget they're human most of the time."

Chris snorted. "Yeah, they're human, all right, and kinky as hell, which is awesome. But I just asked them, and they agreed to it. I think it helps that they were already best friends and cared about each other a lot."

Jaime rubbed her thigh, not sure she wanted to know too much more, but unable to resist asking. "Are Todd and Jim bi?"

"No, they're heterosexual, just like to share." Chris's voice had gone cautious again.

"Wow. I'm impressed. Most guys I've met won't let another dick anywhere near them." She bit her lip and decided discretion was the better part of valor. "I'm curious what it's like to have two men working to please you, but I don't think I want to know so much about your sex life."

"Good, because I don't think I want to give that much detail."

They both laughed with relief.

"Seriously, though, you're okay with it? I don't want it to be weird at barbeques or anything."

"Yeah, I'm fine with it." Jaime nodded. Chris had never been traditional, as evidenced by her choice to become a SEAL, and she appeared no different in her love life, either. "And I'm really happy for you, Todd, and Jim. Jim looked so miserable at the wedding, and I knew he loved you then, but let you go to Todd. Something must have changed after that."

"Yeah, he pulled his head out of his ass." Chris chuckled as male voices sounded in the background. "Hey, I think they just got back from the gym. I'm so glad you're okay with this, but we're not broadcasting it because not all our family members are so open to it. You'll keep it under your hat?"

"Yeah, I can do that. I'll act like it's normal, because

to you, it is, and that's fine with me."

"Thanks, Jaime. You're the best."

"Odd thing to say coming from a retired SEAL." Chris laughed as Jaime meant her to. "I'll report back after my date with Stanton tonight, though I think I'll keep the details to a minimum."

"Thank God. I have enough to worry about with two SEALs. I don't need to know the sexual proclivities of three."

Jaime laughed. "As you say, roger that. Take care and have a fun afternoon, Chris."

"Copy that."

The line went dead and Jaime set the phone down. Damn, that woman had the most exciting life ever. Two men, and SEALs to boot? *It's hard enough for me to find one man who does it for me, let alone a SEAL.* But a small part of her worried about getting involved with a man who led such a necessarily secret lifestyle. Jaime admitted she was all about communication and talking about stuff. SEALs couldn't talk about their lives beyond the on-base training, and sometimes not even that. The idea that her lover couldn't talk to her made her stomach clench.

It's just a date. It might turn out to be nothing more than tonight.

Yeah, she'd be working with him, but if the evening didn't work out, they could remain professional contacts only. But her gut told her the likelihood of that was slim.

"And Slim went home."

Her gut rarely led her wrong. *It's gonna be an interesting night.*

CHAPTER FIVE

Kevin jumped in the shower to wash off the salt brine from the dip he took in the Pacific. After talking with Deli, his frustration still hadn't abated and he didn't want to bring it with him on his date with Jaime. He let the hot water stream over his head and shoulders, mentally releasing all the emotion with the liquid.

By the time he dried off, he'd gotten his mind back in the game and dressed in a light sweater, jeans, and a leather jacket to keep out the January chill. He'd found her office by looking her up on the internet and following the Google Maps directions. The office sat in between an art gallery and a high-end purse shop. Kevin couldn't fathom the need of some women to spend several hundred dollars on a bag for their wallets, but Ghost had once told him it equated to what he'd spend on the best scope for his rifle. He still didn't get it.

The door to her office had a large glass panel with the suite number stenciled in gold letters. Inside a set of stairs led up to a small landing with two doors on opposite sides. The door to the left held Jaime's name and title on it. Kevin knocked and listened as footsteps sounded on the other side.

"Hi, Kevin. Right on time." Jaime smiled as she held the door wide. "Won't you come in?"

He matched her smile as he stepped into an airy loft space over the art gallery. One half of the room held a kitchen and sitting area with plush chairs and a coffee table with magazines spread artfully over its oaken surface. The other half held her office with a large L-shaped desk and filing cabinets. Everything appeared neat and orderly, though a few papers marred the pristine desk surface to the left of the computer keyboard.

"Are you ready to go?" He didn't expect an affirmative, but he'd learned it wise to ask.

"Almost."

He swallowed a groan and tried to cover it with a cough.

"Don't give me that look. I just need to print the contract. Then we can go." Jaime settled in front of the computer and clicked the mouse before her printer hissed out the pages.

"So did you find out anythin' helpful at all?"

"Yeah, actually, I did." She gathered up the papers from the printer and set them on the desk in front of him. "Initial here, here, and here, then sign and date here."

He scanned the contract for any inconsistencies to what they'd discussed, but found it just as clear and straight forward as the woman herself. He signed and dated it then slid it back to her.

"So where d'you want to go for dinner?"

"There's this little Italian place down in old town Coronado. It has a bunch of hanging flower baskets in the summer and a wishing well fountain in a courtyard." She signed the contract and ran it through her copier. "It's called Fontana Dolce and it has the best cannoli I've ever had. Do you like Italian?"

Kevin couldn't answer, the image of Jaime lying on a bed with sweet cannoli cream smeared over her body in strategic locations momentarily stealing his voice and attention. His cock, however, responded with admirable alacrity to his thoughts and he mentally checked the erotic image before he gave too much away.

"Yeah, Italian. Good stuff." Not his smoothest answer, but the best he could do in light of his sudden need to see her naked.

"Good. Are you okay, Kevin?"

"Uh-huh, yep. Good." *Damn, I'm down to one-word sentences now.*

"All right." She handed him some papers. "These are your copies of our contract so you know I know what we know." She winked as she shrugged into her leather jacket. "I have my car here so why don't you follow me to my condo and we'll take your vehicle to old town."

"Sounds good." He followed her out of her office and waited for her to lock the door before leading her down the steps.

Etiquette required him to cover her back, but wisdom taught him to go first, scout the way, and secure their approach. Kevin opened the glass paneled door and stood back to allow her through, all the while keeping an eye on their surroundings. He didn't expect any trouble in the posh part of Coronado, but private investigators didn't always meet with friendly clientele.

She shot him a questioning look, but said nothing as she headed for the parking lot in the rear of the building. Her car sat with three others, the store and gallery clerks working late on a Saturday night in hopes of grabbing some of the art crowd. He waited for her to climb into the driver's seat and close the door before he knocked on the window.

"I'll follow you."

"Okay. What are you driving?"

"Blue Toyota Tacoma." He waved at the building. "Parked in the lateral spaces in front. I'll pull out behind you when you go by."

"Sounds good." She turned the ignition and he patted the roof as she rolled up her window.

He trotted for his truck, pleased he'd get to see her place. *And if I'm lucky, I'll get to see the inside.*

****

Jaime told herself to calm down before she caused an accident on the way home. The traffic in Coronado wasn't bad that night, but she'd reverted to excited high-schooler when she'd seen the royal blue Toyota pickup pull out behind her as she left her office. *He's gonna follow me home! Can I keep him?*

Somehow Chief Kevin Stanton didn't strike her much like a dog. *A wolf or a tiger, maybe, but not a dog.* She wondered if the description applied to him in bed. *I'm definitely gonna find out tonight.* She hoped he wouldn't say no this time.

She parked her car in her designated spot behind her condo and locked it. She wore the same clothes as she had that morning, but she hoped Kevin wouldn't mind. *Get a grip, Hensen. He probably couldn't care less.* She chose not to over think it and trotted for the front of the building where he waited in his truck.

Damn, he looks good. How good would he look in her bed wearing nothing more than a cocky smile? *Easy there, girlfriend.* While he seemed interested, she didn't like to make assumptions about a man's willingness to have sex with her at the end of the night. *You know what assumptions do.* And she'd had a few men run away when the date had ended. Assertive women sometimes scared them, even the ones who seemed so confident.

"Ready?" Kevin gave her a warm smile and his shoulders dropped a little.

Relief? That's a surprise. Reading the micro

expressions from him gave her a leg up. *Maybe that's why the men ran.*

"Yeah, I'm good. Still okay with Fontana Dolce?"

"Yup. Sounds like a good place for dinner. Where is it?"

Jaime laughed as he pulled into traffic and he raised an eyebrow. "Sorry. I half expected you to say, 'got coordinates?'"

"I might if we were planning a mission, but on a date I try to leave the 'operation-ese' on base." He gave her a grin. "So if you'll give me directions to the place we'll head on out."

"Drive to old town and I'll give you more specific directions to the best places to park."

"A'ight." He turned left onto the town's main drag. "So how did you become a private investigator?"

Sadness threatened to take away her breath, but she shoved it aside. She'd lived with it long enough it should've been easily ignored, but aspects still needled her when she thought about it.

"You know my sister went missing twenty-two years ago. I'd just started high school and they'd offered a vocation class on criminal investigations." It had gotten her through Mia's disappearance, the hope that she'd be able to find her when no one else could. "It wasn't very in-depth being offered to freshman and sophomores, but it gave me a focus and the drive to learn anything that would help find my sister."

Kevin nodded. "You must've excelled in it."

"Heh, I did so well, the instructor helped me get an internship with the local police department."

"Whoa."

"Yeah. It was amazing. I didn't get to go to crime scenes, but I helped the techs analyze the evidence and even noticed a few things they hadn't considered." The techs had been so impressed they'd taken up a collection so

Jaime could go to college and get an advanced criminal justice degree with a minor in psychology. "It got me to college when my parents couldn't send me, and it helped me become skilled at what I do now."

"But it didn't help you find your sister."

"Not yet, but I got that gut feeling." Jaime loosened her jaw and took a deep breath. He might not believe in her gut feelings, but she refused to let someone else's doubt derail her. She'd had to deal with such opinions since she started, and one Navy SEAL added to the crowd wouldn't change it.

Kevin shot her a look, but said nothing.

"And you, what made you choose to be a Navy SEAL sniper?"

"How do you know I'm a sniper?" He turned into old town and she waved at the light.

"Take a right at the light."

"A'ight."

"Chris told me when I asked her who you were at the wedding." She shrugged. "Besides, while all Navy SEALs I've met have intensity and focus, the snipers are the ones who get so quiet you forget they're there until they move." Jaime eyed him a little and watched his jaw contract. "You strike me as the kind of man who does a job he can't talk about, but boxes it up and sets it aside so you can still interact with civilians. Turn left up here."

He huffed a laugh as he turned the wheel and she enjoyed the play of muscles in his arms. He kept his hair in light-brown waves curled around his ears at his shoulders. She wondered if it would be soft in her hands when he licked her pussy. *If I can convince him to do that.* She shivered and let her mind fantasize about his body hair. Would it match what grew on his head? *I'll find out when I suck his cock...if he'll let me.*

"Pull into the lot behind the shops here. Best kept secret from the tourists." She pointed to the relatively open lot for a Saturday night.

Kevin deftly maneuvered the truck into an empty spot and turned off the engine. He turned his hazel gaze on her and tipped his head, a half-smile curling his lips as he considered her with no less intensity for all he smiled.

"You seem to know a lot about Navy SEALs."

"I've been with a few."

She smiled, but her gut clenched. A lot of men couldn't handle a woman who made up her own mind about sex and enjoyed it. Many still held onto the outdated belief that men could screw anything, but women had to be pure as the driven snow, an irony considering the men had to screw someone. *I hope he's not turned off because I have a lot of sexual experience.* She'd always been careful for her own health, using both birth control and condoms for her sexual liaisons, but she'd been labeled a slut more than once.

"To be fair, I've hooked up with Marines, too."

Kevin laughed. "Well, at least you didn't go for the Army."

She grinned. "Not intense enough for me." She pushed her door open, suddenly needing the free air to dispel some of the same intensity she'd mentioned.

He exited his truck and locked it before meeting her at the tailgate. "Why Navy SEALs, specifically, though? I'd think we'd be tough to date. We're always gone and we can't talk about where we go or what we do. I've heard a lot of women hate that about us."

Jaime considered as she took his offered arm. *God, I love that old fashioned charm.* "I think what I like most about the SEALs is their willingness to connect intimately for just a short time, a moment of release and relief for them, and for me." She shrugged. "Call it an affirmation of life after those rough, intense times, but the intensity you all carry is heady and exciting, and the sex is unbelievable."

"Damn. You don't mince words, do you?"

She shook her head. "Never saw the need to do so. I'm not a politician's kid, I don't like subterfuge, and I don't play games. Being straightforward has served me better than pussy-footing around. Especially when it comes to sex and relationships of any kind."

"I like that about you, Jaime. And the only one who'll be doin' any pussy-footin' should be me." He winked as he escorted her toward the restaurant.

She laughed and squeezed his arm. *Yes!*

They stepped through the doors and the scents of garlic, tomato sauce, and basil filled Jaime's nose. She loved the old world feeling to the place, and excitement bubbled in her chest with the opportunity to share it with Kevin. She'd never brought anyone else to this place, usually letting them pick the restaurant. But this guy felt special to her, important enough to take him to her favorite haunts.

Guido, the maître d', nodded to her and held up one finger to let her know her table would be ready soon. She'd made the reservation as soon as she'd gotten back to her office that morning. When she'd first discovered Fontana Dolce, she'd just solved the Hollywood kidnapping case and the friendly host had joined her in a celebratory glass of wine for her success. She'd teased him for his first name sounding more like a Mob enforcer than a smooth and friendly restaurateur, and he'd winked with a secret smile. She hadn't learned if this was a 'Family business', but she'd never felt uncomfortable on the premises.

"This is a nice place. Is the food good?" Kevin swung his sharp gaze around the room, taking in the patrons and the servers with equal assessment.

"It's the best. One of my favorite places in Coronado." Guido appeared behind the reservation station and grabbed two menus before waving her past the crowd waiting for tables.

"Damn, how'd you do that?" Kevin escorted her after

the beefy maître d'.

"I called in a reservation, hoping you'd be okay with Italian." She gave a one-shouldered shrug. "Is it okay? Fontana Dolce is really busy on Saturday nights, even if only the locals know about it."

"Yeah. I like a woman who knows what she wants and makes efforts to get it."

His admission warmed her from the inside out and she couldn't help the grin spreading across her lips as Guido showed them to a small back table behind an arbor-like privacy screen. Jaime raised her eyebrows at the owner and he winked behind Kevin's back.

"It's good to see you again, signora Jaime. Who's this handsome fella you're bringing here tonight?"

"Guido, I'd like you to meet Chief Petty Officer Kevin Stanton of the United States Navy." She pulled out her chair and sat while Kevin held out his hand to Guido.

"Nice to meet you, sir."

"Ah, a Navy man and a chief, no less." Guido shook Kevin's hand firmly. "This is good. A chief might be able to keep up with our Jaime."

Kevin raised an eyebrow. "You have a rather low opinion of men."

"Oh no, sir. I have a very high opinion of signora Jaime." Guido smiled and handed Kevin a menu. "What can I bring you to drink tonight?"

"I'll have a sparkling water, please." Guido's opinion warmed Jaime's heart.

"I'll have a local pale ale."

"Of course." Guido winked at Jaime and disappeared into the main room.

"You've definitely made an impression on him." Kevin sat and opened the menu.

She shrugged, a smile curling her lips. "I don't know how. I've never brought a guy here with me."

"Never?" He shot her a look over the menu.

"Nope."

"Maybe that's it, then. I'm honored to be the first."

If I had my way, you'd be the only. The thought surprised her. Normally she preferred the quick hook-up, a wham-whir-thank-you-sir sort of affair. She didn't have time for men who were clingy, or worse, men who expected her to wait for them while they went on deployment. She wasn't a long-term type of woman. Usually.

"I figured you'd appreciate a good hole-in-the-wall Italian place." That sounded plausible and almost relaxed.

"Let me guess. You're the master of the casual, right? Nothin' long term or hopin' he'll call again the next day. Sound about right?"

Jaime blinked as she unfolded the cloth napkin on her lap. "Maybe. How do you know?"

Kevin shrugged as he dropped his gaze to the menu. "A lot of the guys in the squad are like that. Or were until they got married."

"But not you?"

"Not for a while now." He grimaced and pointed at the menu. "Whaddya recommend from this place?"

She allowed him to distract her from his curious response and she suggested the chicken with a creamy pesto sauce, though everything Guido's staff made was delicious. Guido brought their drinks and supported her suggestions while they ordered.

"So why "beta" squad?"

"What?" Kevin's brow lowered in confusion.

"Sorry, non-sequitur. Chris always calls your squad 'beta', but I'm pretty sure the military designation of B is 'bravo.' Where did the title beta come from?"

He laughed. "Chris never told you?" When she shook her head, he nodded. "When Chris got injured and was doped up on morphine, she said we "did it mo'betta" than all the other squads on the team, and Deli, Petty Officer

Rubenovich, pipes up with Beta Squad, and it stuck. So Bravo Squad became Beta Squad, at least to the members."

"Ah, I see. It's an inside joke."

"Yeah, kinda. Though we're not much of a joke to our opponents on missions." His grim smile made her shiver. "The word beta is a designation, not a representation of our skills."

"I don't doubt it." Words had meaning, but in the SEALs' world, actions spoke far more eloquently to their abilities.

Their meal arrived and they both tucked in. To her delight, Kevin seemed to enjoy the food as much as she, moaning with pleasure. *Now I just need to him moan like that when I take him home.* She smiled and kept her thoughts to herself.

Guido appeared beside the table when they'd finished and smiled with approval. "I see you both have enjoyed the meal. Can I get you dessert? We have a marvelous cannoli and an exquisite tiramisu that is the best in the city. It has won the Best Desert for three years running."

Kevin laughed. "Aw hell, can't turn that down. We'll take one of each."

"Can we get it to go with us? I'm stuffed on your delicious pesto, Guido."

"Of course. I'll get that packaged up for you and bring your ticket." He scooped up their plates and sauntered away.

"So what would you like to do now?" Kevin met her gaze, his expression both polite and intense.

"You're asking me?"

He shrugged. "I figured I should ask given you brought me here to your favorite restaurant, a place you've brought no other dates. You're in control tonight, Jaime."

"Oh yeah? A SEAL relinquishing control? Now I've seen everything." She winked.

He chuckled. "At least until you make a decision about

where we're going. I'll take it from there."

The confidence in his voice sent a little thrill through her. She'd been an independent woman since puberty, but some of her fantasies featured a man full of intensity, taking control in the bedroom. While she didn't fancy a relationship in the BDSM lifestyle, she did like her lover to be assertive, all his intensity focused on her. *Yeah, who wouldn't?*

"Why don't we go back to my place? That way we can enjoy the desserts, and anything else, without worrying about sleeping somewhere safe." She wiped her mouth with her napkin to hide her excited smile.

"Well, ma'am, I'd be honored to escort you home and help you enjoy the sweets, and anythin' else." He grinned as Guido returned to the table.

The Italian man paused, holding the check in his hand as he swung his gaze between them.

"Forgive me, who shall I give the check to?"

Jaime opened her mouth, but Kevin held out his credit card. "That would be me. Jaime so graciously brought me to her favorite restaurant and has been willin' to help me on a pressin' matter, I feel I should at least take her out for dinner."

"Excellent, Chief Stanton." Guido took the card and winked in approval at Jaime.

"You didn't have to, you know. I'm under contract after all." She finished her sparkling water.

"Yeah, I know. But I did ask you out earlier and I like to treat a lady." He took her hand and squeezed. "Especially since you brought me to the place you haven't brought anyone else."

"That's a big deal for you, isn't it?"

"Yes, ma'am, it is. It says more than just agreein' to be my date tonight."

Guido returned with the card and Kevin signed it before they took their leave. But before they could step out the freshly painted door, Guido pulled Jaime aside.

"Are you sure, signora Jaime?"

She frowned. "Sure of what, Guido?"

"Sure he's the one? He is in the Navy." The older man's brow creased in consternation.

"The one? As in my knight in shining armor, my hero, the man of my dreams?" She shook her head with a smile. "Don't be silly. He's just my date tonight."

"Ah, signora, I suspect he's more than that. Just be sure of him, eh?" Guido patted her arm. "You're more than enough woman for him, but he must be a strong enough man for you. And being in the Navy isn't a good measuring stick for that kind of strength, capice?"

She opened her mouth to be flippant, but realized his concern stemmed from real affection for her.

"Okay, Guido. I'll be sure of him. But you know you have to break eggs to make an omelet and I have to give him the time to show me who he really is." She patted his arm.

"I just don't want to see you hurt. You're like family, and family is very important." He winked.

"Thank you, Guido. I appreciate it. I'll be careful, but I can take care of myself."

"Yes, yes, I know." He kissed both her cheeks and squeezed her shoulder. "Okay, you have a good night, now."

Jaime left the restaurant and joined Kevin on the street, still flattered and amused by Guido's actions.

"Everything okay?" He took her arm and walked with her toward his truck.

"Yeah." She nodded. "He's just making sure your intentions are honorable."

Kevin laughed. "I don't know about honorable, but they are centered on making you feel good all night long."

"Oooh, I really like the sound of that." She squeezed his arm as her nipples hardened inside her shirt and her pussy spasmed. It had been a while since she'd last enjoyed a man, but Kevin Stanton still represented the one she'd missed. *Not gonna miss him tonight.*

"The goal is for you to like the feel of it, too." He winked as he unlocked the truck's passenger door.

"Bring it on, Chief Rimshot."

CHAPTER SIX

Kevin laughed and his cock hardened in his pants. *Hooyah!* He loved her challenge and directness. Jaime lived up to her words. She didn't pussyfoot around, and he found the trait very appealing. Most of the women he'd met or picked up played coy and shied away from speaking about sex, even in innuendo. But Jaime knew what she wanted and at the moment, it was him. *Hallelujah, and pass the ammunition.*

He wanted to tear out of the parking lot and floor it toward her condo, but he forced himself to drive reasonably through Coronado's streets. Jaime leaned her head on one hand against the truck's door and grinned at him.

"Are you sure you can handle a SEAL, ma'am? We tend to be intense."

"Is that a challenge or a warning, Chief?" She licked her lips and he thought he'd swallow his tongue.

"It's a promise, Ms. Hensen."

"I've been with SEALs before, and yeah, they're intense." She nodded, but her smile never slipped. "But not all SEALs are alike and there are levels of intensity. I'm hoping your level fits what I'm looking for."

"And what exactly are you lookin' for?" He eased off

the gas pedal before he tore through the residential neighborhood just south of hers.

Her silence lasted longer than he expected and he shot her a quick look. The expression she wore reminded him of the one his sister sported when deciding whether or not to tell him her secrets. It was a mixture of caution, apprehension, and revelation, as if she'd learned something new with his question.

Jaime's expression shifted at the last moment and she shot him a sultry smile. "I'm looking for a man who knows when to wait to prolong the pleasure and when to pull the trigger. Know someone like that?"

"Hot damn. Yes, ma'am, I do."

He made it back to her place in less than five more minutes and had the truck in park and the keys in his hand before he knew what he was doing. *Slow down, jackass. You don't wanna scare her off just cause your dick is beatin' against your zipper.*

Although, Jaime didn't seem to be the kind of woman who scared easily. Still, his mama had taught him to be a gentleman, and taking his time with Jaime seemed to be the best way to make them both happy. *And we'll definitely be happy tonight.*

They got out of the truck and Kevin barely remembered to grab the desserts as he watched her sexy ass sway in front of him up the walk. The wind had died down during dinner and Kevin wished it could cool him off as his blood heated with her movements. *Sweet Jesus, she's beautiful.*

"Come on in." Jaime stepped through the door and held it open for him.

The room beyond felt larger than it was as she closed the door and switched on a light. Large sliding glass doors opened into a small fenced backyard with a patio, and a picture window in front helped create a feeling of space. She'd decorated with soft earth-toned colors, reminding him of some of the desert locations he'd visited. *Not that I saw them much during the day.*

The room smelled like Jaime and the spice of pine boughs. He'd forgotten New Year's had happened only a month earlier. Holidays didn't have much meaning when he spent them hunting terrorists.

"Do you want to eat the cannoli now or later?" Jaime licked her lips and his cock flexed in appreciation.

Can I eat the dessert off your sexy body? He reined in his libido enough to seriously consider her question.

"As much as I appreciate a good dessert, I'm not hungry for more food." He set the Italian confections on the kitchen counter and sauntered back to her. "Maybe we can work up an appetite and eat it later."

A wide grin split her lips. "That sounds like a plan. The bedroom's this way."

He paused long enough to throw the lock on the front door before following her up the stairs. She raised her eyebrows as she shot him a look over her shoulder.

"Worried about intruders?"

"No, ma'am, just makin' sure we won't be interrupted. Been waitin' too long for this to hurry it now."

She grinned. "I like the way you think, Chief. The bedroom's at the top of the stairs."

She hadn't been kidding. The entire upstairs had been split into a loft with an attached bathroom. The large space held a queen sized bed, some oak bedside tables and a bureau, and a fluffy chair with a lamp. Skylights gave the room an airy feeling and she'd decorated with sunrise colors to match the earthy tones downstairs.

"Wow, this is a great room."

"You should see it in the morning light."

"If I'm really lucky, I expect I will." He winked at her as he toed off his shoes.

"I'm definitely hoping you will." She sauntered over to him and rested her hands on his chest. "Let's take off this jacket and your shirt. I've wanted to see your chest and back without clothes since the wedding."

Her bold statement made his cock flex, and he shrugged out of his jacket. He pulled the sweater over his head and added it to the jacket before daring to look at her. Jaime's gaze skittered over his body and he swore it felt like a sensual hand on his muscles. Her eyes flashed with arousal and her cheeks flushed as she ran her tongue over her lips in appreciation.

"Damn, honey, you do that again and I'm liable to come in my jeans."

"Well, we can't have that, can we?" She winked and stepped up to him, her hands at his waistband. "Let's take them off before there are any accidents."

He loved her forthrightness and allowed her to strip his jeans from his hips. His cock swelled as she pushed the denim down his legs and she gasped a little to find he'd gone commando. *Hell, I'm SpecOps, she should expect it.*

"Oh, now there's a lovely sight." She licked her lips again and his balls tightened. "Let's get your pants off, then I want a taste."

Did she just say taste?

He had to clear his throat to speak. "Yes, ma'am."

She pushed him backwards until his legs bumped against the bed and he had to sit down. She dropped to her knees between his thighs and grasped his cock at the base with one hand. Her other hand skimmed over his abs, gently thumping against the hard ridges of muscle.

"I love that you have hair only on your belly and between your pecs." She grinned up at him as her fingers tangled in the hair around his navel. "It gives me such a good happy trail to follow straight...down...here." She squeezed his shaft just before she fitted her mouth over the head.

There was nothing so sexy as a woman who had no fear of sucking cock, and Kevin couldn't hold back his moan of delight. The slick, wet heat surrounded his glans and he swore stars erupted across the backs of his eyelids. The hand around his shaft squeezed as her other hand slid between his thigh and his scrotum, rubbing the tightening skin.

"Holy shit, Jaime." He threw his head back as he braced himself on his arms behind him and rode out the pleasure.

She hummed against his taut flesh as she bobbed up and down, her hands distracting him almost as much as her slick tongue and hot mouth. She raised her whiskey-colored gaze to meet his and the edges crinkled as she pulled back enough to lick from his balls to the tip of his cock. He hissed his pleasure as she settled down to nuzzle his balls, giving nipping kisses to the sensitive skin. He fisted the bedcovers as she returned to the crown and slid it all the way to the back of her throat.

"Sweet Jesus."

Jaime swallowed a few times and Kevin had to grit his teeth and think about humping a full sixty kilo pack out over rough terrain to keep his orgasm in check. *Although humping might not be the best word to use at this time.* Pleasure damn near swamped his control and his release threatened to boil up out of his balls.

"Ease back there, honey." He sat up and grasped her upper arms to halt her devious tongue.

She pouted as she pulled off his dick, licking her lips with a sensuous slide. "But I was enjoying that."

He chuckled as he pulled her to her feet. "Yeah, I was, too. But it was gettin' too close for me to last much longer, and I ain't never left a woman unsatisfied my entire sexual life." He grinned at her as her expression shifted to delight. "Besides, you're wearin' far too many clothes for my likin' and I think we need to remedy the situation."

He grasped the hem of her lavender top and pulled it off as he rubbed his dripping dick against the front of her jeans. She gave him a smug smile as she grasped the taut flesh and stroked it again. His brain blanked for a second as pleasure overwhelmed his other senses, but he regained his focus and unbuttoned her jeans, swiveling his hips to remove her grasp.

"Aww." She pouted again, but humor glinted in her golden eyes.

"Now, now, honey, you'll get it back, no fear. You just gotta wait for…" He lost his train of thought when her matched set of lace panties and bra came into view. The color reminded him of sweet plums and brought out the rosy tones of her skin and freckles. "Sweet Jesus, you're beautiful, Jaime."

He hadn't meant to say that aloud, but the sentiment stemmed from the God's honest truth. He'd never seen a woman like her with glorious full breasts and hips, and taut belly and thighs. She was tall, too, tall enough to almost meet him eye to eye at his own six feet one inch of height.

"Thank you. I think the same of you."

"Pardon?" Her statement brought him back to the present after drifting happily in her beauty.

"Beautiful. You're beautiful, Kevin." She skimmed her fingers over his chest and belly again, and his cock reminded him not to be distracted by silly words. "I want to enjoy this beauty some more."

"I'm all for that, honey, but I need a taste of your sweet pussy before I give you more of my cock."

She raised her chin in a sexy challenge. "Why does it have to be mutually exclusive? Ever tried sixty-nine?"

Kevin swore his heart stopped as the image of her sucking his cock while he licked her pussy flooded through his mind.

"Aw, fuck yeah, I've tried it, but not nearly often enough." He grinned as he unclipped her bra with deft fingers. "But I need these pretty sweet nothin's to be off so I can enjoy your silky skin against mine."

Her full breasts spilled out of the bra and she let it drop off her arms as he cupped the sweet mounds in his palms. Her skin was as soft and warm as he'd guessed, and he couldn't help thumbing her nipples until they peaked under his touches.

"Oh, God, that feels wonderful." She threw her head back and thrust her breasts harder into his hands.

Hell yeah it felt wonderful. Soft, smooth skin the color of sweet cream and peppered with rosy freckles filled his rough palms. He hoped he didn't scratch her as he reveled in the remarkable fullness. His mouth watered with the need to taste and he dipped his head, fastening his lips around one delectable peak.

"Oohhhhhh."

She moaned. Her salty-sweet taste hit his tongue and his eyes almost rolled back in his head. *It's fuckin' ambrosia.* He pulled on her nipple, using his hands to fondle the other one so it wouldn't feel neglected. He couldn't get enough of her sweet breasts and had to switch to the other, suckling for the sheer pleasure of feeling her nipple on his tongue.

The scent of her arousal hit his nose and he dropped a hand to cup her mound. He found the lace and paused long enough to drag her panties off her hips. She stepped out of them, using his shoulders for balance, before he returned to running his tongue over her belly and breasts. He replaced his hand on her mound, digging his fingers into the curls around her pussy. Slick, hot wetness greeted his fingers as he rubbed them between her nether lips and she gasped, rocking her hips on his hand.

He pulled back to watch her as he rubbed her clit between his thumb and forefinger. She whimpered and bit her bottom lip, sending the blood barreling to his cock in pleasure.

"Aw, yeah, honey. Rub your sweet pussy on my hand. That's it."

SIOBHAN MUIR

He coaxed her to enjoy, but couldn't hold back from sucking on her nipples again. Watching Jaime revel in the pleasure he gave turned him on more than he thought it would. He'd always been a conscientious lover, making sure his partner enjoyed herself while he got his own release. But he suspected he could make Jaime come and find more satisfaction than he'd ever found in his own orgasms with others. *She's the one I want to hear scream my name in pleasure.*

Kevin slid his hand between her legs and thrust two fingers into her dripping pussy. She gasped and rocked harder, her hands gripping his shoulders. He curled his fingers inside to touch that special spot and when he hit it, she dug her fingers into his deltoids.

"Oh, God, yeah, right there!"

He matched her thrusts on his hand, rubbing her clit with his thumb until she clamped down hard on his fingers inside. She threw her head back as her release cascaded over his palm, soaking his hand down to his wrist.

"Yes, yes, yes, YEEESSSSSSSS!"

She held onto him while she shook with her orgasm, her eyes closed and her nails sunk into his shoulders. He withdrew his hand from her quaking pussy and licked her cream from it as he held her with his other arm. Damn, he'd never seen anything quite so beautiful as Jaime in the throes of pleasure.

Before she'd come down from the ecstasy, he rose and scooped her into his arms to carry her to the bed. She trembled and her breasts jiggled with enticing motions that had his cock saluting. *Soon.* He laid her on the bed and held her while she returned to her body from her trip among the stars.

"I've got you, Jaime, my sweet garnet. Just let it ride." Kevin enjoyed the trembling of her body next to his along with the scents of her arousal and release. "Oh, honey, you're the most beautiful thing when you come."

A shaky laugh fluttered against his shoulder. "Thanks."

"I'm serious." He was. He'd made lots of women come, but none warmed his heart or made his chest expand the way her pleasure had. "Nothing more sexy than a well-pleasured woman."

Jaime laughed again. "Except for maybe a well-pleasured man." She took a deep breath and sat up. "I think we should put it to the test."

"Oh yeah?" He grinned as she pushed him onto his back.

"Yeah." She fitted her knees between his legs and grasped his hips, tracing the edges of his oblique muscles straight to his groin. His cock perked up and flexed just from her gaze on it. "I'm going to start with getting another taste of your hard cock, and then I'm gonna roll a condom over your weapon so I can ride you hard. You think you can handle that, Chief?"

"Honey, I can handle anything you give me. I'm a SEAL after all." *Even your heart.*

The thought shocked him so much he inhaled in surprise, but fortunately his reaction was covered by her lips sliding over the head of his cock.

"Oh, hell yeah, Jaime. Suck my cock hard, honey."

She chuckled around his taut flesh and he saw stars once again. But instead of the long, drawn out blow job, she only teased him with her hot mouth and tongue this time. When she pulled back from him, he couldn't help the whimper of dismay, even as she pulled out a foil package and slid a condom over his flesh. She crawled up his body to straddle his hips.

Jaime grasped his shaft and positioned the head at the edge of her slick nether lips. "Are you ready for me, Kevin?"

"Hooyah, ma'am."

She grinned as she sank down onto him, but it turned into a grimace of ecstasy as if she hadn't expected the pleasure of his intrusion. He certainly hadn't expected her to be so hot, slick, and tight. He'd never worried about the size of his cock before—Nature gave him what She did—but her pussy gripped him like a hot, steel glove and his eyes rolled back in his head from the erotic pressure. *Sweet Jesus, she's so fuckin' sexy.*

"Oh, god, yeah." Her breath sighed out as her breasts swung above him. "Damn, you're big and I love it."

She set the pace, slow and easy, her clit dragging along the length of his shaft, and he lost his ability to speak. He held her hips and reveled in the rolling motion of them over his cock. The scent of her arousal filtered into his nose as her soft groans matched each thrust. He grasped her breasts and sucked on one of them as she leaned forward to brace herself on her hands over him.

He'd always thought he preferred to be on top, but watching Jaime take pleasure in grinding her pussy on his shaft turned him on more than ever before. His cock solidified inside her and his hips increased the friction between them by rocking into her thrusts. The orgasm she'd teased him with built up to a screaming pitch and he gritted his teeth to hold it back a little longer.

A little bit longer, son. Just until she tips over the peak.

"Oh, god, Kevin, I'm going to come. Oh, oh, oooohhhhhhh!"

Her pussy clamped down on him so hard he didn't stand a chance. With her clit rubbing a line of erotic fire on his shaft and her pussy muscles squeezing like a vice, his release boiled out of his balls and shot him into the cosmos with a roar. His mind left his body and the world behind, and his heart made one clear and firm statement.

Mine.

Deep, heartfelt understanding settled in him as he floated in the euphoria of his orgasm. *Jaime is mine and I'll never give her up.* He slowly came back to his body as Jaime rested on his chest, her pussy still wrapped around his softening cock. His breath sawed in his chest, but the scents of warm, satisfied woman and sex filled him with deep satisfaction. This was the moment he'd remember most when on missions far away from her sleepy, sexy body.

I love...this. The last hadn't been the word itching to materialize in his consciousness, but it was the only one he was comfortable thinking at the time. Anything more was too soon and too much.

"Thank you." Jaime whispered the words into his neck after brushing his skin with a soft kiss. "That was wonderful."

He chuckled. "Get some rest, honey. Because I ain't done with you yet tonight." He squeezed her gently as she raised her head to look him in the eye.

"You're not?"

"Oh, hell no. SEALs can go all night. We're built for endurance."

She snorted and smirked. "This isn't a mission, Chief. This is supposed to be sex and romance."

"And I plan such ops with the same careful attention." He winked as she giggled and slid off him. He pulled the condom off. "Right now, I plan on cleanin' that sweet pussy of yours and cuddling with you until we're both ready for another round. Then I'm gonna love you all over again." He rolled off the bed. "You got washcloths up here in this bathroom?"

"Yes. In the linen closet right inside the door."

"Thanks." He found them and headed for the sink, dropping the condom in the trash. Satisfaction settled into his gut. He'd wanted to do this with Jaime for months, and he wasn't about to let the opportunity to love her end early. This was a night she'd never forget. He'd dig himself so deep in her heart she'd never want anyone else. With that happy thought, he returned to the bed to care for his woman.

CHAPTER SEVEN

Jaime ran her hands over her face as she sat back in her chair with a groan. Frustration ran like ants with little spiked feet through her mind, sparking anger and despair in alternating patterns. She wanted to scream or weep, depending on the moment, and instead she leaned her head back and closed her eyes.

Six weeks had passed since she'd brought Kevin Stanton home and enjoyed his very sexy body. He'd been a helluva lover and true to his word, had stamina to make love with her several times that night. Fortunately the next day had been Sunday and she'd been able to rest up.

Their relationship had progressed. *Yeah, that's the best word for it.* They'd gone out many times and had sex as often as they could, but though she enjoyed being with him and his mind-blowing lovemaking, the rest of the time he became the glacier. He showed her nothing on the outside except during sex and she found herself in the unusual position of needing more. And knowing she couldn't have it even if he would give it to her.

Thus the territory of dating a SEAL. She growled and rubbed her neck. *I want more communication than "hey, my dick's hard, that means I love you."* He hadn't ever said the L-word and she didn't need to hear it. Really. *That's my story and I'm sticking to it.*

So she'd thrown herself into her work, alternately researching Bethany Stanton's disappearance and her sister Mia's. While Kevin went on various missions with the SEALs, Jaime focused on tracking down the McMackens in the Army. It kept her from worrying about whether or not the chief would come home.

Captain E. Roger McMacken had been in Afghanistan at the time of Bethany Stanton's disappearance. He had seen many strange things during his tour, but he'd never heard of SNAIFU and joked along with her at the idea of supernatural anomalies of any sort. He seemed like a nice man and she thanked him for his time.

General Sean L. McMacken almost refused to talk to her, but finally admitted he'd been in a series of Department of Defense fiscal year meetings for all of September and October of the year Bethany disappeared, and several others corroborated his story. *So not him either.*

Ian and Tabitha McMacken had been much easier and far friendlier to contact. They were down-to-earth people with a wicked sense of humor, but she sensed deep sadness in both of them. *Probably about their daughter.* She'd asked them about Killian's Ford Tenpenny and they'd said they'd recently sold him to the Sagittarius Wildlife Sanctuary in Wyoming. She'd written it down, though something seemed hinky about a quarter horse breeder selling a champion stud to a random wildlife sanctuary in BFE Wyoming. Especially one without a phone line or internet, only a post office box in a nearby town. All her instincts flashed the warning semaphores and she made a note to check on the owners.

She'd chatted a bit more to find out about their son and where he'd gone after he was discharged from the Army. Hesitancy and reserve entered their voices and she suspected she'd hit something. They mentioned he'd recently gotten married to a nice gal and lived in Wyoming on an old historic homestead. When she asked where, they'd made vague references to northeastern Wyoming and the town of Gillette. She'd thanked them and decided to do her own research.

"At least that's going better than my relationship with Kevin." The bitterness in her voice echoed in her empty office space.

She loved so much about Kevin. His drive, his focus, his intensity. She adored his need to protect the country he loved and devote all his time and focus to it. And when he loved her, it was nothing short of magnificent.

But everything was good, glossed over, and distant. *And that's the problem.* She understood SEALs couldn't talk about where they went or what they did. She didn't expect him to, but she did expect him to let her in on how he felt or what he needed beyond sex. She wanted his attention and his intensity, but she also wanted to connect with him on a more casual and mundane level. She wanted to hear about the non-classified mishaps or events of his training days. She didn't expect him to be ordinary, but she wanted him to let her into his world, even if just on the fringes.

Instead he'd bottled it all up and given her nothing.

She'd finally confronted him with it, pushing him to show her something, anything about how he felt or what he wanted from her. Hell, she'd have settled for a nervous admission of his affection. But he'd retreated into his cold and stoic "Samurai Mask" and refused to say anything. She'd told him to get the fuck out until he could give her more than what he showed terrorists. He'd blanched white and left. Jaime grimaced. *It's my own stupid mistake.*

She'd cried, actually cried over a man, for three days, but every time she thought to text or email him, she'd reminded herself of all the times he'd shared nothing with her and her anger would reignite. *I won't live a half-life. I don't care how much my heart wants him.*

Fortunately, during one of her weaker moments, a contact came back with some information on a mysterious company called Data Pool. Located in Columbia, it supplied everything from office personnel to medical equipment and clothing. Kind of a Wal-Mart of South America. But something seemed as hinky about Data Pool as it did for the McMackens to sell a champion quarter horse stud.

Looking into their records, Jaime noted almost all the personnel were young women between the ages of eighteen and twenty-seven. While she applauded affirmative action, she found it questionable that many of the women seemed to leave the company within months of being hired, and disappear completely. Almost all of them came from the United States, though a few came from Canada and the surrounding South American countries, but none of them had any connective information beyond that listed on the company's website. No Facebook, Twitter, Instagram, or Google Plus accounts in any of the women's names.

According to their events schedule, the Data Pool held hiring fairs geared toward women and offering classes and training in everything from electronics to med-tech skills. *Were they in Kentucky at the time of Bethany's disappearance?* She wrote the question down on a sticky note to check and stuck it to her computer screen edge. She then scanned the executive officers of the company, surprised when she found the CEO was a woman in her thirties with strawberry blonde hair and brown eyes. The name on the site read "Mercedes Hermanas de Olvidado". The image remained too grainy to see her features clearly, but Jaime's gut did a little dip. *That looks like Mia.*

She shook her head and made a note to check more thoroughly on the origins of the CEO.

It took her a few more days, but public records yielded the names of the owners to the Sagittarius Wildlife

Sanctuary as Stephen P. and Bethany A. McMacken. There were no photographs associated with the purchase documents, but they'd only been in Wyoming a little less than a year. Jaime made calls and checked the official website for pictures of the owners. The woman had lightened her hair a little and wore clothes more suited to being a ranch hand rather than a senator's daughter, but Bethany McMacken was definitely Bethany Stanton.

Jaime sat back in her chair and rubbed her eyes with the backs of her hands, sighing. A couple of months' worth of work and she'd found the wayward senator's daughter. *Alive, thank God.* Jaime studied the picture of the couple. They looked happy and relaxed, settled. She had no idea why Bethany had disappeared and neglected to tell her family where she'd ended up, but at least Kevin would know.

Jaime sighed as she picked up her phone to text him. They hadn't spoken or communicated in more than cryptic texts in over the last few weeks, but she'd tried to keep him abreast of her investigation. *He might be an incommunicative jerk, but I'm not.* She grimaced as she typed out her text to him.

Found Bethany. Meet me tomorrow morning at the Island Breeze Café at 0800 for full disclosure.

She hit send and glanced at the clock. The digital numbers read 22:47 and she shook her head. She'd changed it to military time to understand Kevin when he said he'd be returning from or leaving for training. *I should really change it back to civilian time.*

She reached for the clock, but checked herself when she heard a sound behind her. She turned as something reflected in the screen of her computer, but before she could do anything, a thick arm snaked around her throat and squeezed.

Jaime tried to inhale as she thrust her feet against the floor, surging upwards against her assailant. The man grunted and tightened his hold as she threw herself to the side in an attempt to dislodge him while her arms scrabbled at the limb around her neck.

When he wouldn't release her, she used her remaining strength to thrust her elbow backward into his gut. But the lack of air made black spots swim in her vision and dissolved her strength. Before she blacked out, she hoped her text to Kevin made it through and maybe, just maybe he'd come looking for her.

CHAPTER EIGHT

Kevin sat beside the entrance to the Island Breeze Café at 0755 sipping his coffee with the first sense of hope he'd had in seventeen months. Not only was Jaime talking to him—well, at least texting—but she said she'd found Bethany. *Take that, you SNAIFU morons.*

If he was totally honest with himself, he'd admit most of his relief came from Jaime's willingness to contact him. After their fight, he'd abided by her wishes to stay away from her, but it'd damn near killed him. Going on training ops and other missions had helped, but when he had down time, his mind latched onto her sultry smile and her auburn hair.

He swung his gaze to the front as the doors to the café opened, but a balding man stepped across the threshold. He checked his watch. *Only 0759. Calm down. She'll be here.* He still heard her anger and frustration when he didn't show emotion on his face. She wore her heart on her sleeve and he didn't have to guess how she felt or what she thought. She was the most transparent woman he'd ever met. And part of that scared the shit out of him. She didn't hide how she felt about him or how much he'd come to mean to her. She told him, flat out, she'd started to love him, to want him. They'd become a couple in her mind and he hadn't known how to deal with it.

Despite the fact you want the same thing, jackass.

Kevin checked his phone as the door to the café opened again, but still no sign of Jaime. *Where the hell is she?* She'd never been even a few minutes late. They hadn't talked more than short texts, and he wrote it off as part of his missions and operations. But she'd burrowed under his skin and he missed her more than he should.

He tapped out a new short missive. Did you forget our appointment? He frowned at his flippancy and deleted the words before he came across as an asshole. Are we still on for 0800? I've missed seeing you.

He hit send before he could take it back and relaxed in his chair to wait. But as the minutes ticked by, his gut warned him something was wrong. *Don't be a nervous Nelly. There's nothing wrong.* Except, she wasn't texting him back and his neck itched.

Finishing his coffee, he dialed Jaime's number and dropped a few bucks on the table, his worry overwhelming the discomfort of speaking to her. *She'll probably chew me out for my punctuality and I'll have to apologize.* But her phone went to voicemail and the cramp in his gut worsened.

"Hey Jaime, I know we haven't talked much, but I was just wonderin' where you were. We were supposed to meet this mornin' at the Island Breeze Café, right? Anyway, just hopin' to touch base with you. Give me a call when you get this."

He shoved the phone in his pocket and headed for his truck. Something wasn't right. He slid into the driver's seat and turned over the engine. *I'm probably just jumpin' at shadows.* He dropped his phone in the console as he pulled into traffic, telling himself he had nothing to worry about. But as more time passed and Jaime didn't text, dread took hold in his gut. He'd heard of the sensation and the emotion, but he'd never experienced it until now.

Pulling up in front of her office, everything appeared serene. He grabbed his phone and jumped out of his truck, taking in any odd details. It was too early for the shops around her place to be open, but the door to the stairs showed gouges where someone had forced their way in.

Swallowing the urge to shout, he pulled the door open and listened. Nothing moved upstairs. Kevin shoved his keys into his pocket and wished he had his Glock on him as he took the stairs two at a time. He paused at the landing and held his breath, listening again. An ominous silence filled the spaces between his heartbeats and he wrapped his hand in his t-shirt to grasp the doorknob. It turned without a sound and he pushed the door open.

Aw fuck.

The room on the other side lay in complete disarray. Small items like plants and pencil holders lay scattered on the wood floors. The chair behind the desk had toppled and the desk itself had been wiped clean. The laptop he'd seen there was missing and papers decorated the floor. The bookshelves stood empty, their contents lying on top of the papers.

"Aw hell, Jaime." The words echoed in the still air, half prayer, half admonishment.

Kevin stepped carefully around the mess of papers and personal debris, looking for anything to give him a clue to who'd taken her. He found her phone on the floor, the battery removed and the face broken as if someone had stomped on it. *Guess she won't be getting my texts.*

He stepped back and glass crunched under his heel. He dropped to his haunches and picked up a picture frame with the snapshot still buried in the broken glass. Jaime and her older sister back when they were kids. They looked happy, carefree. She'd said it was the best memory she had of her sister Mia.

Kevin swore and looked around for something to wipe

down the frame. It wouldn't do for him to leave his prints here where the cops could find them. He rose and picked his way across the floor to the little kitchenette, hoping a dish towel would be handy. His mind already started categorizing the damage he'd seen, and while he wasn't a trained crime scene detective, his gut said the destruction seemed personal.

He found a towel inside the cabinet door below the sink and wiped down the frame and the door handle. His gaze snagged on a bright yellow sticky note stuck to the bottom of his shoe and he lifted his foot to remove it.

The words 'Bethany', 'Data Pool Co.', 'South America', and 'kidnapping?' caught his attention. He yanked the little note off his foot and read it more thoroughly. According to Jaime's notes she wondered if Bethany had been kidnapped by a company in South America. She'd told him in a text she'd found his sister. Maybe she'd gotten too close and Data Pool didn't want her scrutinizing their daily operations.

Kevin dropped the picture frame on the cluttered floor and tossed the towel onto the counter. He picked his way through the debris as he yanked his phone out of his pocket. They needed intel on Data Pool and what the company did, because he had a feeling it would lead to Jaime and Bethany. *Two birds, one stone.* He just hoped the birds still lived.

****

"You were right. There's something 'hinky' with Data Pool and it's been on Department of Homeland Security's watch lists for a while now, according to the intel." Deli brought up the information on the computer screen. "When did you start using that word, anyway?"

"From Jaime."

"Oh."

It was no secret he'd been dating the lovely private investigator, but no one knew they'd broken it off. At least, Kevin hadn't told anyone. All they knew was she'd been kidnapped and the company she'd been investigating seemed the likely culprit.

"From what intel found, these folks tend to have 'hiring fairs' for almost exclusively women, which the equality movements in this country favor." Todd grimaced as he read through the printouts. "Unfortunately, these fairs seem to be for the company to accumulate young women, determine their value to them, and then 'hire' them. But they're disappearing. No social media accounts, not even for the 'long term hires'. Definitely hinky."

"Aw hell. Jaime's note said she thought they'd taken my sister Bethany the last time they were in Kentucky." Fury rose, but Kevin held onto it. "I knew she was going for her veterinarian's degree and this company has a vet's internship program. If I was a bettin' man, I'd say that's when they got her. Where is the company located?"

"Looks like... the town of Cali, about eighty klicks in from the west coast of Columbia." Jim pointed the map on Deli's screen. "And nothing between the coast and the town, which means good cover for insertion if authorized."

"That's the first good news we've gotten." Kevin nodded sharply.

"Oh yeah, how's that good?" Greg raised an eyebrow.

"Because now we can go in and get them out. It ain't domestic soil."

"No one's gonna okay us to go down there just because you're girlfriend's been taken." Greg scowled and shook his head. "Which fucking sucks."

"My girlfriend isn't what'll give us the go-ahead. It's my sister." Kevin grabbed his phone and headed out the door into the parking lot. Hope bloomed in his chest. *Time to step up and be a man, Senator Stanton.* It was a long shot, but he'd insult the hell out of his father's manhood if necessary to get what he wanted. *You're not the only one who learned to manipulate, you smug bastard.*

"Stanton residence." A woman's voice, roughened by years, answered his call.

Kevin looked at his phone, certain he'd called his father's cell number. "Rosemary? It's Kevin Stanton. Why are you answering my dad's cell phone?"

"Kevin, is that you? My stars, it's been a coon's age since I've heard from you." The woman who'd served his father for years snorted. "And I'm not answering his cell, he's forwarded the blasted thing to the house phone again."

Kevin laughed at her frustration. "I'm glad I got to talk to you, Rosemary. It's been too long. And I'd be happy to catch up, but I have a time-sensitive matter I need to discuss with my father. Would you be willin' to track him down and have him answer? It's very important."

"I'll do that if you promise you'll call me back when you have more time and maybe even come home for Thanksgiving this year."

"If you're cookin' your famous sweet potato pie, I'll put in for leave this instant."

"Note to self: sweet potato pie brings Kevin home. Got it." She chuckled. "Let me track down the Senator."

Kevin couldn't suppress the grin. Rosemary came across as submissive and deferential to his father and anyone who came to see him, but she knew how to play the game. She subscribed to the idea that the man might be the head of the household, but the woman represented the neck and could turn the head any which way she chose. Kevin wouldn't have believed it if he hadn't seen her do it.

"This is Senator Stanton." His father's voice came on the line and Kevin bit his tongue on the remark that he'd lost his senate seat over a year earlier.

"Good afternoon, sir. It's Chief Petty Officer Kevin Stanton. I need to speak with you on an urgent matter concerning your daughter."

A short silence ensued before Stanton responded. "I see you've deigned to call home because of it. What do you want, money?"

"No, sir." Apparently his father had forgotten the trust fund Granddaddy had set up for Kevin—a fund the elder Stanton couldn't touch. "Somethin' much easier. We got intel that Bethany's been abducted by a company that supplies young women for black market uses such a sex slavery, organ transplant sales, tissue samples, and whatever else you can think of."

"Have you confirmed that, Chief? I can't get mixed up with scandals like that."

Even when it's your daughter, you lousy sack of shit?

"Yes, sir. We need your connections in the Pentagon and the DOD. We need you to make an order for SEAL Team 9, Bravo Squad to go in after her." Kevin didn't let his voice change inflection, even if his heart beat a nervous tattoo inside his chest. "Now that there's a political target, there can be a legal order to send the SEALs in."

"Why should I make such an order to endanger American lives?"

"Spare me the political rhetoric, Senator. There are already American lives at stake here. The lives of young woman from across the country, Bethany's in particular." Kevin paused then brought out the Howitzer. "Besides, think of what kind of hero you'll be for going after your daughter when it's discovered by the press that she's been abducted." *And I'll leak it, you prick.*

Stanton sucked in a surprised breath and Kevin knew he'd scored. His father valued nothing more than money except his political and public reputation.

"Think of it, sir. The SEALs go in, pull her and whoever else is there out, and you return all those scared women to their families. You'll look patriotic as hell and the media will be all over it when we do the job right this time." He didn't bother to mention SNAIFU. "Win-win for everyone."

"This is no game, Chief Petty Officer."

"No, sir, it isn't. It's life or death for these women. That's why I'm askin' you to call in some favors to send in the SEALs. Call it a need to protect national security, whatever makes you look good. I don't really care how it gets done, just that it does."

"Why should I do this?"

Kevin ground his teeth to keep his voice even. "Because it's the right thing to do and because it's family. Wasn't that part of your platform every time you campaigned? Family is important, you said. So put your money where your mouth is, sir. You owe it to Bethany for all she did for you. Hell, you owe it to Mama. And you know she's watchin' you."

"Those are big words coming from you, boy." Stanton's voice had grown hard. "What have you done for your sister lately?"

"More than you'll ever know, sir, because the SEALs aren't in the media any more than we have to be and we like it that way." Kevin took a deep breath before he told the old man to fuck off. Popularity was Stanton's thing, not Kevin's. "If you put in the order, sir, I'll be able to do more. Help me save them, Senator, and you can take the credit."

The silence on the other end of the phone stretched and Kevin closed his eyes. *Please, Mama, if you're listenin', kick the senator in the ass and get him to do something right for his daughter.*

"I'm sorry, Chief. I can't help you."

The line went dead and Kevin almost threw his phone across the parking lot. *You goddamned motherfucker!* He gripped his cell phone tight and took a few calming breaths before he felt ready to face the rest of the squad. He honestly had no idea what to tell them.

He was still struggling to rein in his fury when Deli

strode outside. The shorter man stopped beside him without a word and they brooded in silence for several minutes.

"Bad news?" Deli's voice sounded casual.

"The motherfucker won't do a damn thing for his daughter, and I got nothin'." Kevin had never been so close to tears. "All we need is someone to get the Pentagon to give the order to go in. That's it. And he won't do it." *I'm so sorry I was such a reserved prick and wasted all that time without you, Jaime.*

Deli didn't say anything for several minutes while Kevin wallowed in his furious impotence. The SEALs were the best in the world, but they could be easily derailed by conscienceless pricks worrying more about money than people.

"There might be a way." Deli dropped his chin and rubbed his upper lip with one finger. "Rick from the GAPS crew was bitching about one of his partners always being busy with his girlfriend when not glad-handing people."

"So?" Kevin tried to rein in his surliness. *Damn, I sound like Bam-Bam.*

"So the girlfriend is one Missy Greenwood, daughter to Senator Greenwood."

"The guy looking for the presidential nomination?"

"That's the one." Deli nodded. "Let me contact Rick and see if he can get his teammate to light some fires. It's a long shot, but it might just work to get us wheels-up."

"Do it."

Deli nodded again and headed off to make his call while Kevin let hope replace the fury. It was all in God's hands now. *Which fuckin' sucks.* He hated not being in control, but at this point they needed divine intervention. He threw his head back and shot his gaze to the sky.

Please, God and Mama, if you're able to move these folks in the right direction to save Jaime and all the other women, I'd be awful grateful.

He hoped someone was listening.

CHAPTER NINE

Jaime slowly swam back to consciousness, though her head hurt so much she rather preferred to remain out of it. But sounds and smells intruded into her awareness and she took a chance to open her eyes.

She lay on a daybed beneath a window in a tastefully decorated office. The window sat cracked and a warm breeze, too warm for winter, billowed the gauzy curtains hanging at the end of the daybed. Turning her head, she caught sight of cherry bookshelves towering above a matching desk with a computer and a few office supply knickknacks strewn over the surface. A tall potted plant held court beside another wide window and the sounds of distant city traffic floated in with the breeze.

She appeared to be alone, but she didn't want to sit up yet to find out. She couldn't hear voices or the tick of fingers on a keyboard, but each pulse of her heart sent pain throbbing through her head and she couldn't hear much of anything. The cotton dryness of her mouth suggested she'd been out long enough to be dehydrated.

Where the hell am I?

The air smelled humid and tropical, very different from the wetness of Coronado. Jaime tried listening for birds or gulls' cries, but nothing familiar came to her ears. She scanned the ceiling of the room and studied the smooth plaster between the artfully rough-hewn beams. Someone had spent a great deal of money to make the room appear homey in a place of business.

Not gonna learn much by lying on my back.

Taking a deep breath, she pushed her body up into a sitting position. Her head throbbed to beat the band, but resting her elbows on her knees helped settle the pounding. She breathed slowly, focusing on the inhale and exhale until the thudding faded enough to hear herself think.

When she could turn her head without pain screaming at her, she took in more details. The office reminded her of all the fancy businesses of wealthy clients she'd visited who'd wanted to be discreet when searching for their missing illegitimate children or the mother of said children. She tried to think of anyone she'd pissed off enough to enforce her kidnapping, but she couldn't think of anyone.

She'd only been working on Bethany Stanton's case.

Maybe her father is pissed I'm bypassing the Army?

But the air didn't smell like Kentucky in the winter any more than it smelled like Coronado. Maybe she'd pissed off the Men In Black who didn't want her knowing about SNAIFU, dragging her off to somewhere like the prison in Guantanamo Bay. Jaime glanced down at her clothes. *No orange jumpsuit.* And the office was far too sophisticated to be a prison warden's space.

She wanted to look out the windows to determine if she'd recognize any landmarks, and gathered her strength to test her ability to stand. Before she could move, the door to the office opened and a woman strode in.

Jaime's first impression was of power and confidence. An eggplant purple tailored suit ending in a mermaid skirt covered sensuous and robust curves. Dark blond hair had been pulled into a stylish up-do, held in place by two black lacquered chopsticks, and black low-heeled pumps covered her feet. The woman strode to the desk and neatly seated herself in the leather chair, her nails clicking on the keys of the keyboard. She never said anything to Jaime, her focus on the monitor in front of her.

Jaime blinked. *So I'm just another throw pillow on the couch?*

She straightened her shoulders and cleared her throat. "Excuse me, but where am I?"

The woman at the desk paused in her typing, but didn't turn around for a few heartbeats. Jaime had no idea what she could be thinking, but she seemed to be wrestling with some sort of dilemma. *Yeah, whether to keep ignoring me or respond.*

At last, the blond turned to face Jaime with a distant, professional smile. "You're in my office, Jaime."

Jaime had been confused before, but now the bottom fell out of the world and her jaw dropped with it.

The years had changed the figure and lined the face, but the eyes remained the same rich brown under arching brows. She hadn't seen the familiar configuration of the features in twenty-two years, but the woman sitting behind the desk could be none other than her older sister Mia.

"Mia?" Jaime gaped, all her thoughts scattering.

"That's right. Have you forgotten your older sister?" The voice was smooth and older than she remembered, but still held the same cadence she recalled from high school.

Jaime blinked, trying to comprehend what she saw. "Never, Mia. I've never forgotten. I've been looking for you for decades." She tried to get up, but her body protested with pain and weakness. "What happened? Where have you been? Are you all right?"

"Aren't you sweet?" The sarcasm dripping from Mia's voice could've poisoned drinking water. "So interested in what happened to me, yet never having done anything about it. Your concern is touching."

"What are you talking about?" Jaime's anger made

inroads through her surprise. "I never gave up trying to find you. I've been searching every day since high school."

"Yes, but you were just a kid. What could you know about missing persons?" Mia tilted her head to look down her nose at Jaime. "But the others, Mom, and Bill, and my so-called *friends*. None of them did anything. I was abandoned, ignored, forgotten. Even the cops gave up after a few months, didn't they? Better things to do, I'm sure. I knew no one would be there to save me. I'd have to save myself."

Jaime clenched her hands into fists, willing her body to get up, but it remained too weak. "Tell me what happened, Mia. Tell me where you've been."

Mia snorted and sat back in her chair, crossing one leg over the other. "Oh, now you want to know?" She shook her head. "I think it's pretty obvious. I was kidnapped, abducted, but not by aliens. At least not those from outer space. These aliens were small-time thugs from Mexico, hired by the head of a Columbian cartel to find blonde-haired girls for his sexual stable."

Jaime gulped. "Oh, God. Were you raped, Mia? Did he hurt you?"

Mia dipped her chin and shot her a dry look. "Really? I was stolen to be included in the bastard's sexual stable and you ask if I was raped?"

Jaime shoved the anger back behind her eyes. "How did you get out of it?"

"What makes you think I did?"

Jaime shot her own dry look back at her sister and waved at the office around them. "This isn't exactly a padded cell with a bed for forced fucking."

"My, my, my, you've grown to have a mouth on you." Mia shook her head with reproval, but she smiled. "Eventually I figured out a way to kill him. He never saw it coming and I did it before I got too 'old' for him. No one would ever abandon me again."

The hair on the back of Jaime's neck rose at the gleam of unbalance filling Mia's eyes, but the serene mask slid over her face again and she smiled sweetly. "But his death left a vacuum in a very lucrative business and I had nothing, so I took over to give myself something to do. Turns out I'm very good at business." Her gaze hardened again. "Bill was wrong about me being useless with money."

Jaime blinked. Bill had been their mother's husband at the time Mia went missing. He'd been a drunk, an asshole, and smarmy as hell, but he'd cared for their mother until Mia disappeared. It became rather evident he'd only cared for Mia. *And by 'cared', I mean sickly sexually interested.* Jaime suppressed a shudder. She thanked God to have been born a redhead. Bill preferred blondes like her mother and Mia.

"Are you saying you run a business? The business of the cartel that kidnapped you?"

"Yes." Mia's smile turned smug as she leaned her elbows on the desk, her fingers laced. "And I've expanded it. Now instead of just blonde-haired girls, anyone has an opportunity to work for Data Pool. We've won best international employer of the year from Women's Magazine four years running."

"And the women you 'employ', what fields do they go into?"

"All fields. We have great programs in the medical fields like obstetrics, gynecology, genetics, organ donation, and medical sciences." Mia's professional smile took over. "We supply our clients with domestic engineers at all levels from housekeeping, cooking, child care, and professional companionship like hospice care. Our employees are utilized in pharmaceutical trials, chemical engineering, and medical testing like makeup and tissue samples."

All that sounded great, but Jaime had briefly looked for Mia's employees, and none of them seemed to exist beyond what her company put online. The problem was Jaime didn't know this Mia and she didn't trust her any farther than she could spit. She tried a different tack.

"Why didn't you ever contact me to tell me where you were? That you were alive?"

"I wasn't alive, Jaime." For a moment, lucidity showed in her sister's gaze. Aching anguish stared out from a deep well of despair. "Mia died years ago when I became forgotten and abandoned."

"I never abandoned you, Mia. I've looked for you every day."

Mia scowled and snorted, the madness returning to her eyes. "It doesn't matter."

"It does matter. It mattered to me." Jaime beseeched her with her body language and her expression. "I never gave up on finding you, Mia. You were the motivation spurring me on every day to find others who'd gone missing."

A cold smile quirked Mia's lips. "I imagine some of them were those my men took."

Jaime's stomach dropped and she swallowed against bile. "Let's get out of here, Mia. Come home with me. We'll be together finally and we'll get you some help—"

"I don't need help!" Mia rose and leaned on the desk, her eyes blazing. "And there's nothing for me there. Here I'm the master of my own universe. I have money, I have power, I have respect, and I love what I do. Mia died decades ago. Mercedes Hermanas de Olvidado took her place and has thrived."

She paused and tipped her head. "You could join me, you know. There's a place for you here. You'd never have to worry about making money or searching for anyone again. And we could hang out."

Jaime saw her pretty, vivacious sister for an instant, the person with whom she'd shared the fashion magazines and Halloween candy growing up. Jaime wanted her sister back so badly it brought tears to her eyes.

"I already make money. I have a thriving business, Mia. And I help people."

"Thriving?" Mia snorted, her expression contorting into contempt. "A measly hundred and twenty grand a year, max? And that's if you have a client each month. Please. Here, you could make ten times that much, easy."

Jaime straightened, testing her body for mobility. Whatever she'd been drugged with had started to wear off. *Just a little longer.*

"You've been checking up on me?"

Mia shrugged. "Ever since we got wind of your searches about our job fairs and programs, I've been aware of you and your little private investigator service." Her nose crinkled with disdain. "It's cute. Seriously, though, you could make far more money here with me."

"Off the backs of others. Where are all those women you 'hire', really, Mia?"

"I told you, they're trained in our programs and sent to clients all over the world."

"Spare me the sales pitch. I'm not buying." Jaime held up her hand. *Hey, at least I can move it now.* "Tell me what you really do with them."

Mia shrugged. "We utilize them wherever there's a need."

Jaime's gut churned. "Utilize them? They're not office supplies, Mia, they're people."

"Oh, I beg to differ." Mia's smile turned dark. "They're used for cancer and genetics and drug testing. Tissue samples, gene therapy, organ donation, cadavers for medical schools, household staff, and sex toys. If there's a demand for a special kind of woman, we supply her to the client. It's all part of the services we provide. And the feminist groups sing our praises because we help women only. In a male dominated world, we're heroines."

"Heroines?" Jaime couldn't hide the horror in her

voice. "You're stealing women away from their families and selling them, Mia. They never agreed to it."

"Oh, they agreed. They sign on with the company to fill whichever capacity we need at the time." Mia's voice grew cold. "It's all perfectly legal and they're grateful for the opportunity." Her expression turned beseeching. "There's a place for you here, Jaime. We could work together and make lots of money. You'd never be poor again."

"This is crazy, Mia. You can't do this to people." Jaime tried her own persuasion.

"They aren't people, they're product. And there's a good market for it."

Oh my God. The woman behind the desk wasn't Jaime's sister. Sometime in the last twenty-two years, the loving person Mia had been had died, just like she'd said. A monster who saw women as tradable merchandise had taken her place, dressed in designer suits as she pretended to be a reputable business manager.

"I'm sorry." More than Jaime could say. "I'd never do this. It's wrong and horrible. Stealing women from their lives is sick."

For a split second, Mia's professional façade cracked and unmitigated rage flashed across her face. But it disappeared as swiftly as it had come, and she gave a sharp nod.

"Then our business here is done." She picked up the phone on her desk and had a short discussion in unaccented Spanish. When she hung up the phone, she gave Jaime the original serene mask she'd worn coming in. "It was good to see you again, Jaime. I'm sorry we couldn't work out an agreement."

Jaime rose, grateful she had the strength to do so. "Please, Mia, don't do this. Let these women go."

Mia shook her head sadly. "My name is Mercedes Hermanas de Olvidado, and I decide how this company is run, and how we distribute product."

The doors to the office opened and Jaime turned to see who'd entered. Two large men who looked more like thugs than businessmen entered the room. They each had black hair, dark brown eyes, and richly tanned skin. Mia rattled off something in Spanish to them and before she could react, the men had grabbed Jaime's arms and pinned them behind her back at painful angles.

"Please take our newest acquisition down to the holding cells and make sure she's not damaged. At the moment I don't have an order for a redhead or her tissue type, but I'm sure we can find some use for her." Mia's professional serenity never cracked. The rest of the instructions were delivered in Spanish just before Jaime felt the prick of a needle in her neck.

"Ow! Mia, let me go! You can't do this. I'm your sister."

Whatever had been delivered into her system took hold almost immediately, and her muscles turned to Jell-O. Mia shook her head.

"I don't have a sister, Ms. Hensen. Thank you ever so much for coming. Best of luck."

Then the world went dark again.

CHAPTER TEN

Kevin mentally fist-pumped. Deli's contact at GAPS whipped out a miracle within twenty-four hours. Senator Greenwood pulled whatever strings necessary to get orders from the Pentagon mounting a rescue op to recover Bethany and any other innocents from their alleged kidnappers. Intel provided preliminary printouts of Data Pool's headquarters located in Cali, Columbia, with maps to old catacombs beneath the newer structure. The company had an extensive network and connections, most of which were legitimate, but each time Kevin thought of the group, his gut dropped and his rage rose. Things were definitely hinky.

Armed with DOD orders and intel, Beta Squad went wheels up and headed for the USS Sussex, an LHD2 Wasp class amphibious assault ship berthed in San Diego. Moving fast and quiet, they reached the Pacific international waters west of Colombia in less than ten hours. By the time the engines slowed, Kevin had stripped and reassembled his rifle three times and gone over the plan more times than he cared to count.

I'm coming, Jaime. We'll get you and Bethany out.

"Locked and loaded, Rimshot?" Retro bumped fists as

they loaded the CV-22B Osprey on the rainy deck of the Sussex.

"Hooyah, LT."

"Good. We're two men down on this op and Ghost is gonna be pissed if we don't come home, so watch your sixes. The new guy doesn't come in until next week." Retro tapped his cheek mic.

"Timing is everything." Bam-Bam snorted.

"Roger that. We're going in at 2200 hours, near-dark, and most of the workforce is headed to a late dinner or already home. Remember it's summer there this time of year." Retro pointed to a map he'd unfolded on his lap as the bird lifted off the deck. "The building abuts the forest. There's a cliff overlooking the compound here to the northwest. That's your high ground, Rimshot."

Kevin nodded.

"We go in along the west perimeter fence and search for captives in the catacombs below ground. Deli." Retro pulled out a schematic of the building. "You need to get to the server room with Bam-Bam. Intel wants their files."

"Roger that." Deli nodded as he pocketed the flash drive allowing remote wireless access to the electronic vaults.

"Once you've planted Intel's toy, head down to the basement to help with evac and setting charges with Bam-Bam. Command said "scorched earth" for this one." Everyone raised eyebrows and Retro shrugged. "Bury the bodies with the evidence once we get the innocents out. Bam-Bam, can you bring the building straight down?"

Killian nodded as he checked the schematic. "Yeah, LT, I think so. Hit the right support posts and that sucker will collapse in on itself."

Retro nodded. "Good. Magic and I'll take point. We evac the targets, then bring the building down. Rimshot will cover our retreat."

"How many targets do you think they have inside?"

Deli looked up from securing the flash drive.

"Heat signatures last put twelve downstairs, but it wasn't clear how many were guards. Keep an eye out for Jaime Hensen and Bethany Stanton. You all clear on appearances?"

Retro had asked this many times before, but no one shot him a sarcastic look. "Roger that."

"Fifteen mikes to LZ." The voice of the pilot came over their headsets.

Retro nodded and raised his fist. Everyone mirrored him and spoke the oath they repeated before each mission.

"Keep low, move fast. Kill first, die last. One shot, one kill. No luck. Pure skill."

"Hooyah!"

The rest of the flight was spent checking gear and getting into the mental space. Kevin closed his eyes and let himself sink into Rimshot the sniper, his Samurai Mask sliding over his face. He shoved his worry, fear, and fury behind a thick wall of cold stillness, the place from which he drew his concentration. By the time they'd reached the LZ and dropped into the gathering dark, he'd become the glacier the Squad claimed he was.

The Osprey wheeled away in the sky, leaving fast and quiet. Retro's voice came across the coms reporting all boots on the ground. They waited for a confirmation from the pilot then Retro signaled for everyone to head to their planned positions. Rimshot took off for the high ground overlooking the buildings in the valley below.

The warm, humid air filled his nose and lungs as he moved through the forest into position. He found a flat spot on a large chunk of granite overlooking the compound surrounded by shrubs without thorns or poisonous spines. *Thank God for small favors.* He set to making a nest and threw a camouflage net over himself as he crouched. He screwed the suppressor onto the barrel of his rifle and settled belly-down between the bushes.

"High ground in position. I got eyes on the compound, over."

"Roger that." Retro's voice settled into his ear like a comforting touch. "ETA four mikes to fence line."

"Roger that." Rimshot kept his gaze through the scope and caught the movement of his squad just before something else moved into view. "LT, be advised. Pair of guards heading your way at your nine o'clock."

"Copy that. We see them. Stand by."

Rimshot waited, watching through the scope as the men approached the squad.

"Take the shot."

He breathed out, closed his eyes, then opened them as he gently squeezed the trigger before shifting just enough to squeeze again. The rifle bucked in his hands with a soft spitting sound and the two men never heard what hit them. They crumbled into the waiting hands of the squad out of camera range.

"Confirmed targets down." Magic's voice entered the coms.

"Affirmative. Moving out." Retro signaled to the squad.

"Roger that."

The squad dragged the bodies of the guards into the bushes outside the fence and headed across the compound. Rimshot watched their progress and took down three more guards before the squad made it inside the building. *Now I wait.* Normally, he was content to sit up high and watch for trouble, removing it before the squad had to deal. But this time, he wanted to be with them to find Jaime and Bethany. The idea that either of the women could be injured made his fury and fear scream loud enough to be heard outside the cold silence, but he ruthlessly squashed them. There'd be time to panic later.

"Catacombs found. Entering now."

"Copy that, LT. Searching for server room." Deli's

whisper confirmed breakup of the squad.

"Roger that."

Come on, give me some good news.

The seconds ticked by in quiet relentlessness. Rimshot forced his shoulders and arms to relax as he watched the compound through his scope. No one had discovered the missing guards or come to investigate yet, but he expected more than just five for a place like this. Sure enough, another pair came from the other direction at the same moment Deli reported reaching the server room.

Rimshot took a deep breath as the guards discovered the hole in the chain link fence and let it out slow before squeezing the trigger twice. Both men collapsed into the shadows beside the fence. Not exactly invisible, but still less noticeable than in the center of the compound.

"Two more guards down, LT."

"Roger that." Retro's voice confirmed his report. "Catacombs breached. It's like a fuckin' prison down here." Soft sounds of suppressed gunshots echoed over the con. "Three guards down. Commencing search."

Rimshot held his breath, but kept his eyes glued to the scope. *Come on, Retro.*

"Server breached. Intel wireless drive deployed. Keying sequence now." Deli's report loosened some of the tension arching through Rimshot's body. "Gateway sequence keyed. Heading for base supports to rendezvous with hostages and set charges."

"Copy that. Two hostages found so far. Neither are required targets."

Rimshot's gut sank at Magic's report. *Fuck, where are they?* Motion through the scope caught his attention and he swung the view upwards to the top floor of the building. Light blazed in one of the upper offices and he had to switch the view on his scope to accept the new spectrum.

"Be advised, activity occurring on the top floor office of building." He focused down to see who was working this late. "Two females and three males in northwest corner."

He studied the men, all three in suits. One appeared to be a wealthy businessman, smaller in stature and wearing diamond jewelry on hand and ears. The other two men looked like his thug bodyguards, big, tough, and prone to violence. *Except when facing SEALs.*

He shifted his view to the women. One dressed in a smart suit, red in color, with matching lipstick and heels. Her blonde hair draped around her face in artful tendrils. *Looks like the CEO.* The other had auburn tresses cascading around her head in loose waves and she swayed on her feet as if drugged or incapacitated in some fashion.

Rimshot's breath froze in his chest. *Jaime!*

"LT, be advised, one of the required targets is being held in the top floor office, northwest corner."

"Fuck. Roger that. Only four hostages down here. Deli, break off and come help Magic escort the hostages to the exit. Bam-Bam, set the charges. I'm headed to upstairs. Rimshot, cover my six."

"Copy that." Rimshot swung his scope around the compound to check for more guards. "Compound clear. Evac open." He raised his view back to the office and his teeth ground together as the CEO of Data Pool gripped Jaime's head by her hair and jerked it back.

The smallest man in the office gave a lascivious smile and nodded. The CEO pushed Jaime into a chair and strode to the desk, clicking on the computer. For a moment, her brow creased as she read something on the screen, but she smiled and nodded at something the man in the suit said.

"Retro, have you reached position?"

"On my way. ETA two mikes."

"Be advised, two males to the right of the entrance, one seated on couch your two o'clock."

"Can you take the shot?" Retro sounded breathy as he ran the stairs.

"Negative. Not without alerting the targets."

"Stand by." The sound of a door opening echoed over the com and Retro took a deep breath. "On top floor. Proceeding to northwest corner office."

"Copy that. Have eyes on occupants and standing by."

He waited, watching the office as the woman behind the desk retrieved some papers from the printer. His heart thundered in his chest, but he breathed slowly, focusing on the tableau in the scope.

"Breaching office."

"Roger that."

Though he couldn't hear much, the view inside the office changed dramatically. The two thugs dropped like heavy boulders before they could even get their weapons from the holsters. Mr. Sharp-Dressed-Man had enough time to get to his feet and blanch white before Retro's bullets took him in the chest in a tight mass. But Ms. CEO had pulled a nine millimeter from somewhere and now held the muzzle to Jaime's head as she jerked the redhead in front of her as a shield.

Retro and the CEO froze in a standoff with Jaime between them.

"Rimshot, take the shot."

"Say again, LT?" Rimshot's gut froze. Was he insane?

"Take the shot, Chief."

"Negative. Do not have clear shot."

Dread hit him like a bucket of ice water as the woman with the nine mil raised her chin in challenge. *Dear God, no.* He had to make a decision. *Hell, Magic, I hope your sorcery is with you tonight.* He took a deep breath and dropped the muzzle of his rifle. *I'm so sorry, Jaime. Please forgive me.*

He inhaled slowly to calm his speeding heartbeat and closed his eyes. When he opened them, he aimed, exhaled, and squeezed the trigger.

****

Jaime knew something was wrong, but the world had gone all fuzzy and soft. Her sister hugged her from behind with one arm, but something cold pressed against her temple. *She's not giving me a wet willy, is she?*

A man in black fatigues with matching grease paint on his face stood just inside the doors. He held a Glock nine millimeter pointed at her, his expression serious, but she thought she recognized his features. *Is that Chris's Jim?*

"Take the shot, Chief."

What shot? Like 'hit me with your best shot?'

"This is what you're here for, isn't it, soldier boy?" Mia spat her words as her grip on Jaime tightened. "Well, you can't have her. She's mine to do with as I—"

Searing white-hot pain exploded in her abdomen at the same time Mia shrieked and released her. Shock broke the strength of her legs and she collapsed on the floor with a heavy thud. The blood roared in her ears as a gunshot cracked in the deafening silence of the room. Plaster from the ceiling sprinkled down on her as the man in black fatigues darted between her and Mia. Another crack from a handgun and silence reigned.

God it hurts to breathe. Why does it hurt?

"Ms. Hensen, my name is Lieutenant Waters with the United States Navy. I'm here to take you home, but first I need to verify who you are."

"Verify?"

"That's right. Can you tell me your mother's maiden name?"

Jaime closed her eyes and thought hard. "G-guthrie."

"Good." Velcro tore apart and hands peeled back her shirt from her abdomen. She gasped and whimpered, and he breathed an apology under his breath. "Can you tell me who your best friend is married to?"

If she didn't hurt so much, she would've frowned and snorted. "Todd Hunter and Jim Waters." She only belatedly remembered Chris had told her to keep that information on the down-low. "Oops."

An uncomfortable chuckle echoed over her head as he wrapped something tightly around her ribs. Jaime moaned and tried to get away from the painful pressure, but she couldn't move.

"I didn't know she told you that."

"Wasn't supposed to say."

"We'll keep it between us." The blackened face appeared in her blurry vision. "Let's get out of here. It's not safe and you need medical attention." He hoisted her up and she whimpered, but the idea of staying in the hideous room with her evil sister sickened her more.

"One target acquired, but she's wounded. Magic, stand by for triage. Deli, Bam-Bam, report."

Jaime stumbled along with the man who smelled like sweat and warm nylon. He seemed familiar and her slow mind helpfully supplied the idea that Chris's Jim had come to rescue her. *Why didn't Kevin come? Isn't he a SEAL too?*

They got into an elevator and he pressed the button for the first floor. Jaime sagged against him while he talked to someone invisible. *Is it a ghost? Could be his wife whose nickname is Ghost.*

"Copy that. Almost to the first floor. Coming out of elevator one. Rimshot, cover our sixes. Deli, call the bird. We'll need transport for ten. I repeat, transport home for ten."

The doors to the elevator opened and two thugs came around the corner. Lieutenant Waters twisted to put her behind him and sent a barrage of bullets from his Glock into the men ahead of them. Both thugs fell before they had a chance to get their guns into position and Waters hustled her past their still corpses.

Jaime stumbled and her feet dragged a few steps. She remembered she needed to stay awake and keep moving, but she'd lost the memory of why.

"Stay with me, Jaime. We're almost there." Waters' voice comforted her and gave her strength, but her body shifted into rebellion.

"I'm sorry." Blackness crowded her vision and she lost her grip on his clothes.

"Aw hell. Magic, I need backup now. Loading docks."

They'd made it to doors to the loading bay, but her legs folded under her and she slid down his body. He holstered his sidearm and caught her before the ground could. "Stay with me, Jaime. You gotta stay awake a little longer, all right?"

"Trying…" She clung to awareness with teeth and nails, but the ringing in her ears swelled to something resembling the clang of Notre Dame's church bells.

The world twisted on her and pain hit her nervous system as Waters hauled her up onto his shoulder in a fireman's carry. She heard his voice talking to someone else as he ran through more doors and out into the night. *How can he run carrying my heavy ass?* Other figures moved in the darkness, but she'd lost the ability to differentiate them.

The low *whup-whup-whup* of rotors against the air hit her hearing just before Waters laid her on a vibrating surface. A new face filled her vision and she recognized Chris's other husband, Todd. She tried to smile, but her face had stopped working.

"I'm tired. Can I sleep now?"

"Yeah, darlin'. You go ahead and rest. We got you covered." Todd patted her shoulder before he went back to work on something out of her sight.

"Okay, good." Jaime let go of everything in favor of the quiet darkness, grateful the SEALs could take over from here. *Just wish Kevin was here.*

CHAPTER ELEVEN

Kevin sat in a hospital room festooned with flowers and balloons and watched Jaime sleep. She looked pale and drawn, but her heartbeat monitor beeped strong and steady, and her breath remained even. Still, she wouldn't have been in the bed if he hadn't shot her. *God, I'm so sorry, Jaime. Please forgive me, honey.*

Guilt ate at him despite the knowledge that he'd done the right thing. The CEO of Data Pool, Mercedes Hermanas de Olvidado, had used Jaime as a human shield in a standoff with Retro. The only available shot was through Jaime. Retro had finished the job with a bullet to Mercedes's head, but Jaime had lost a lot of blood on the trip to the Osprey, and Magic just managed to get her stabilized before she was transported to the infirmary on the Sussex.

The other hostages suffered from drug use and malnutrition, but they'd been cared for and returned to the States for treatment. Bam-Bam also sustained injuries to his arm. He'd been surprised by two of the security force while setting the charges on the building. He'd managed to kill them before he set the timers on the charges and high-tailed it out of the basement. Rimshot had covered their retreat to the Osprey, taking out the last foolhardy guards hoping to kill the hostages. The building had gone up in a fiery light show minutes after they boarded.

Jaime snuffled a little in her sleep as she took a deep breath, and Kevin bit back a smile. She wouldn't like to know she snored. He held her hand as he watched to see if she'd wake up. Recovery from blood loss and trauma took a while he'd been told, but it seemed interminable when it wasn't on his body.

Another deep breath and Jaime opened her whiskey-golden eyes, focusing on him immediately.

"Kevin?"

"Hullo, sweetheart. I'm here."

She blinked a few times as her mind caught up with the present. "Where's here?"

"You're home in Coronado Medical Center. You're back in the U.S."

"Oh, good." She frowned for a moment and he suspected she searched her memories for continuity. "Did the SEALs come to get me or was that a really elaborate damsel-in-distress dream I had?"

He laughed more in relief than in humor. "No, honey, that was all real. Beta Squad came for you."

She frowned harder. "Did I get shot?"

He swallowed hard as the smile fell off his face. *Aw hell, what do I tell her now?* The truth seemed like the only thing he could offer, even if it would suck, hardcore.

"Yes, ma'am, you were." He took a deep breath as he squeezed her hand. "I'm very sorry, Jaime. It was the only way to take out your captor. I'm the one who shot you. Please forgive me."

Silence reigned for several minutes as she processed what he'd said and his gut sank. Her gaze never left his face, but her own version of the Samurai Mask settled over her features. He couldn't read her expression and that scared him more than when she'd shown him everything.

Panic and dread built up in his chest and tears started in his eyes. *Please, God, let her forgive me. I can't lose her now.*

"Please say something, Jaime."

"You shot me."

"Yes, ma'am."

"You shot me to save me?"

He nodded. "It was the only way to protect you and Retro, and get us all safely home to the clear water."

"Isn't that rather counterintuitive? Bullets kill, not save."

He scanned her face for humor, but the mask remained in place.

"Yes, ma'am." He felt like a kid who'd gotten caught breaking a chair to mend a fence.

"Where did I get shot?"

"Through the side, near your right hip. It was a through-and-through, and did minimal damage." *Thank God.* He'd worried it tore her apart when she'd lost consciousness on the bird, but Magic assured him the shot was clean.

"Minimal damage." She repeated the words, anger simmering under her statement. "How on earth is a gunshot wound 'minimal damage'?"

His mind flashed through the statistics of what some of the military's bullets could do to a body, but he didn't think now would be a good time to explain. Instead, he gazed at her with gratitude and dread mixing in his chest. Gratitude that her soul remained in her body and dread that she'd tell him to take a hike. He couldn't lose her again. The time away from her and her kidnapping had crystallized the understanding that she held his heart, more so than even his sister. Kevin had never begged for anything in his life, but he'd get down on his knees and plead for her forgiveness and understanding if it meant she'd stay with him.

I love you. The words he'd only ever said to family. He cleared his throat and dragged his courage out of the footlocker.

"I can't answer your question, Jaime, because there's nothin' that can explain what I did. All I can ask is for you to forgive me because I've never been so scared as when I had to make the decision to shoot through you." He swallowed hard, but plowed on. "I'm hardheaded and stoic, and sometimes so stuck in my head, I forget folks can't read my thoughts or feelin's from my face. But when I was away from you after you told me to get the fuck out, it felt like my heart had been ripped from my chest and I couldn't focus on anythin'."

She blinked, but said nothing and he swore his heart shriveled a little more.

"When you disappeared, I swear I went insane. Hell, I even begged a favor from my father, and I won't go to him for anything." He squeezed her hand. "But I'd go to hell and back for you, and I'd do anything to make you safe." He paused and screwed up his courage as if facing another Hell Week. "Because I love you. Please forgive me, honey."

Jaime's eyes widened and her eyebrows went up. "What did you say?"

He wanted to pretend she needed him to repeat the forgiveness phrase, but he was smarter than that.

"I love you, Jaime."

"You love me?"

"Yeah, even when I'm stuck in my head and won't share what I'm feelin' with you." Kevin grimaced and swallowed against the unreasoning fear of exposure. "I'm tryin' to be more open with you. I know bein' with a SEAL is hard in the best of times, and it's gotta be a hundred times worse with a SEAL sniper, but I need you, Jaime. You keep me grounded and present instead of in my head. And I need that. I need *you*. You've dug your way into my heart and I'm lost without you."

He leaned forward and pressed a kiss to the knuckles

of her hand. "I know I didn't give you enough before, but please let me make it up to you. Please, Jaime. I'm beggin' you."

She scanned his face for a few moments and he held his breath.

"Well shit." She whispered and a sardonic smile quirked her lips. "It's not right to let a SEAL beg." She squeezed his hand. "I'll let you make it up to me, Chief Rimshot, and I'll let you in on another secret."

"What's that?" Hope had already started to bloom in his chest.

"I love you, too."

Before he could stop them, tears spilled down his cheeks as joy poured through his soul. "Oh, thank you God."

He surged to his feet and wrapped her in his arms, burying his face in her loose hair. Relief and gratitude flooded out of him in great sobs and he couldn't stop them for several minutes. He didn't show emotion to anyone, but Jaime wasn't just anyone. She was his heart and soul.

"Hey, now, I've got you. You're safe with me, Chief." She held on to him and let him drench her hair with his tears. "I love you, Kevin. Just don't shut me out, okay? Talk to me when you can. That's all I need."

He sniffled as loudly as a toddler with a cold, but he nodded and sat back down in the chair he'd vacated. "Yes, ma'am, I promise to try."

She gave him a mock-scowl. "Do or do not, there is no try."

He laughed. "Yes, ma'am, Yodette."

She grinned. "And don't you forget it. But I am serious. When Jim Waters brought me out to the helicopter, I was so disappointed it wasn't you who'd saved me. I'll have to get over my damsel bullshit."

"Oh, I was part of the team who went in to save you. We brought out you and the four others we found." He sighed and shook his head. "But we never did find my sister Bethany in Data Pool."

Jaime raised her eyebrows. "Of course not. She wasn't there."

He paused and blinked. "What? Where is she?"

"On a wildlife sanctuary in Wyoming."

CHAPTER TWELVE

Kevin held onto his frustration and anticipation as he and Jaime bounced along the rutted dirt road leading to the Sagittarius Wildlife Sanctuary just outside of Sundance, Wyoming. She frowned as they hit a particularly rough bump and he grimaced, slowing the rental.

"Sorry, honey."

She'd healed for the most part, but the soft-tissue bruising and trauma still pained her from time to time.

"It's okay. I don't think you have to hurry. She doesn't know you're coming so she won't be running away."

"Yeah, I know, but I've worried about her for the last eighteen months. I'm not interested in waitin' much longer to see her." He shot Jaime a nervous look. "You're sure it's her?"

Jaime laid her hand on his thigh. "I'm sure."

Motion out of the corner of his eye made him shift his gaze to a herd of antelope bounding away from the noise of the truck. Ahead of them sat a little stone house in the middle of a wide plain of grasses. Devil's Tower, a large volcanic neck, filled his rearview mirror as they skidded to a halt in front of the house, spraying gravel and slushy snow from the tires.

A man and a woman stood on the front porch, their expressions guarded.

"Try not to be too scary intense, okay, Chief?"

"Yes, ma'am." But he'd make no other promises, especially if the man ahead of them had done anything to his sister.

Before he could do more than scan the house, Jaime got out of the truck and pulled her woolen beanie tighter on her head. Kevin cursed under his breath and slid into the windy morning. He strode around the front of the truck, glad his heavy leather jacket was zipped to his chin. *Damn, it's cold out here.*

He made one last scan of the environs before his gaze stopped on the woman on the porch. While she wore clothes more suited to a ranch than a senator's mansion, she carried herself with the same strength and grace he remembered from home.

"Bethany! Where the hell have you been for the last eighteen months?"

"Subtle, Chief. Real subtle." Jaime shot an apologetic smile at the porch.

"And who are you?" The man on the porch crossed his arms over his chest as he took a step toward the railing. He moved just like an experienced SpecOps operator and Kevin tried to rein in his frustration.

"Chief Petty Officer Kevin Stanton. I'm Bethany's brother." He raised his chin. "Who are you?"

"Major Stephen McMacken, U.S. Army retired. And I'm Bethany's husband."

"Gentlemen, let's not have a cock fight right here in the yard." Bethany stepped forward. "Your lady looks cold and we have hot coffee inside. Why don't y'all come in and we can talk about this without all the posturin' and pissin'." She gestured to Jaime. "Come on inside, honey. Do you take cream with your coffee?"

"Yes, thank you. I'm Jaime Hensen, by the way."

SIOBHAN MUIR

Jaime made her way to the porch and took the stairs slowly.

Bethany frowned. "Nice to meet you, Jaime. You have something ailin' you?"

"Yeah. I'm recovering from a gunshot wound. Still a bit tender."

Kevin lost the rest of the conversation as the women disappeared inside. His gaze never wavered from McMacken's and he wondered what his sister was doing with an Army puke. Jaime had told him McMacken was the CO from SNAIFU and he had to admit the man looked capable. *Definitely not your typical Army officer.*

"You're really married to my sister, Major?"

"Yes, I am." He tilted his head and narrowed his eyes. "Are you a sniper in the Navy?"

"Yes, sir. How'd you know?"

The major snorted. "I've been around enough SpecOps guys to recognize the breed."

"Mack! Let my brother in and you can strut around in the warmth." Bethany's voice carried sharply from the house behind him and Mack grunted with humor.

"Yes, ma'am. Guess I better do as the lady says. Come on in, Chief. Let's see if we can both win back into your sister's good graces." Mack held the door for Kevin.

"I'd say she needs to get back in my good graces. She's the one who's been missin'."

"Yeah, about that. If you're good at keeping a secret, we might just be able to tell you a story."

Kevin snorted. "Secrets are part of the deal when it comes to the military. I have my own set."

"Not like this. Come in." Mack closed the door to the wind and headed across the small rustic sitting area to join Bethany in the kitchen.

The space was small and definitely had the "homesteader" vibe, but it also felt warm, welcoming, and comfortable. He could see hints of his mother's influence in the décor and some of his tension settled. This definitely

114

wasn't just the Major's home. Bethany had chosen this place herself.

"Sit down before you hurt yourself, Kevin." Bethany pointed at one of the chairs in the sitting room as she held out a cup of coffee. "You still like it black, right?"

"Yes, ma'am." He took the proffered mug and settled beside Jaime on the small loveseat made from smooth pine boles and softened canvas upholstery. "How are you doin'? Any extra pain? Need me to get your meds?"

As much as he needed to hear from his sister, she apparently had a husband to look after her and he wasn't going to ignore Jaime ever again. *Lesson fuckin' learned.*

"No, I'm good for the time being. Thanks for asking." She gave him a warm smile and squeezed his free hand before she switched her gaze to the others. "You said you have an extraordinary tale to tell us. We have a little bit of one, too."

Bethany grabbed her own coffee mug, handed one to Mack, and sat down on one of the chairs matching the loveseat. "Given that bullet wound you're sportin', I'd say it's gonna be a doozy. But how 'bout you tell us how you met."

"Jaime's a private investigator specializin' in missin' persons. I hired her to look for you." He narrowed his eyes at his sister. "And she did, but she says you've been here at least six months. What the fuck, Bethany? Why the hell didn't you contact me and where the hell have you been?"

****

Jaime grimaced. Kevin had been fairly patient up until now, but he'd pretty much reached the end of it. She just hoped she wouldn't have to try to slow him down because she was still in the middle of healing and it would be a bitch if she tore something.

"Fuck, even a goddamned text would've been

somethin'." Kevin rose to his feet and Jaime worried he'd punch something.

Bethany sighed and shot a look at her husband, guilt tightening her mouth. *That's interesting.* Mack gave quick nod and she straightened her shoulders.

"We were under orders from the Army to disappear, but I wrote you. Mack's executive officer was supposed to mail it to you." Mack nodded again.

"I didn't get a fuckin' letter!" Kevin rounded on his sister. "You told his parents." He jabbed a finger in Mack's direction. "Hell, they sold Killian back to you. What the fuck, Bethany?"

"I'm sorry, Kevin." Her face crumpled and she wrapped her arms around herself. "Mack's parents knew because the Army debriefed and honorably discharged him. I really did write you, but I didn't want Daddy to find me."

"I'm not the senator." Kevin's lips pulled back from his teeth in a snarl. "I wouldn't have told him where you were. We're family. Why the hell didn't you come to me?" The hurt in his voice made Jaime's stomach ache, but Bethany's chin came up.

"Did you know Daddy wanted to marry me off to his fuckin' toady Coolidge so he could get my trust fund monies?"

"What?" Kevin blinked.

"Oh, left that bit out, did he?" Bethany glowered, her temper overcoming her guilt. "There was a clause to my inheritance. Everything would go to my husband if I married before I turned thirty, so Daddy had the perfect man in mind to finance his career. Bet your inheritance isn't dependent on you gettin' a wife, now, is it?"

Kevin stared at her, his mouth shut in a tight line.

"Yeah, that's what I thought." Bethany shook her head. "I wrote you a letter, but I never heard back from you. I didn't make further contact because I knew they'd be monitorin' everyone, includin' you. Even though I'm thirty and Mack and I got married, I knew he'd fight me every step of the way. I didn't want him to find me until I'd used my money for what I wanted. A place to live undisturbed, doin' what I wanted to do."

"But what about the horse? Won't they find you now because of him?" Jaime touched Kevin's thigh, urging him to sit back down. "That's how I found you."

Bethany nodded with a grimace. "Probably. I used my trust fund to finish my vet's degree and buy this land, but I did it through a blind trust. That's why I had the McMackens wait to sell Killian to the sanctuary. The trail would be cold and the connections muddled." She shrugged. "If Daddy finds me now, he can't do a damn thing. Too much time has passed."

"Fuck." Kevin's fists balled on his thighs.

"I'm sorry, Kevin. I should have followed up when I didn't hear from you. I just figured you were too busy savin' the rest of the world. I never thought you'd still be lookin' for me. Especially after I wrote that letter." Bethany bit her bottom lip as Mack wrapped a supportive arm around her waist, his expression guarded.

Jaime squeezed Kevin's arm. "She's safe now, and like it or not, the past can't be changed."

Kevin's Samurai Mask settled over his features and Jaime held on, letting him process the information. She didn't know what he'd do, but she understood his sense of betrayal. She'd felt the same thing when she first saw Mia again.

At last, he inhaled deeply, his stoic mask relaxing. "It's gonna take me a while to absorb everythin', and I can't promise I won't be pissed at you from time to time, but I'm glad you're okay." He tipped his head. "So where the hell have you really been? Seriously?"

Jaime recognized he was done with chitchat. He'd waited eighteen months to find her and they both wanted to know why she couldn't be located.

Bethany sighed and shot a look at Mack. "We have to tell them."

Mack growled. "It's so top secret, not even the President knows, Beth. Hell, they probably won't believe us anyway."

"We don't have to tell the President. But we have to tell my brother." She laid a hand on Mack's hip where he stood beside her chair. "He's family and he deserves to know. Wouldn't you feel the same if it was Tricia?"

Mack scowled. "That's a low blow."

"No, it's the truth and you know it."

"What's up with Mack's sister?" Jaime tilted her head, her gaze switching between Bethany and her husband.

"She's gone missin'." Bethany nodded at Jaime's indrawn breath. "Oh yeah, and the story is just about as crazy as ours. But one thing at a time. And after you hear our story, maybe we'll hire you to find Tricia."

"I'll help any way I can." Jaime nodded. "Anything for family because family is important."

"Speakin' of which, is the ring on your left hand an engagement ring?"

Jaime wanted to know more about their adventure, but Bethany's expression told her the subject was still a guarded secret. Jaime lifted her hand and rubbed the delicate gold filigreed ring with her opposite thumb.

"Yes, it sure is." She beamed at Kevin and his face relaxed into a smile. "He asked me the day I got out of the hospital."

Bethany squealed with joy and threw her arms around her husband. Mack laughed and some of his tension melted away.

"That's the best news I've heard in a long time. Almost better than Daddy losing the election."

"Not a fan of politics?" Jaime raised an eyebrow with her smirk.

"Not a fan of *his* politics. That man has been in there

too long and he's a right fine bastard." Bethany shrugged. "Any man who thinks he can choose a husband for his daughter in this day and age is a dinosaur that needs to go extinct."

"Hooyah, sister." Neither Jaime nor Kevin mentioned Mia who'd tried to sell her to a man with a fetish for redheads.

"Yeah, well, he doesn't know where I am and I'm good with that." Bethany paused. "You won't tell him, will you, Kev? I'm happy here and I'm doin' what I want to do."

Her SEAL fiancé shook his head. "Nope. As far as former Senator Stanton's concerned, his daughter disappeared, and only Beth and Stephen McMacken live out here takin' care of antelope."

Bethany's shoulders slumped in relief and she approached Kevin's chair. "Thank you, big brother." She held her arms open and Kevin stood to accept a hug.

Jaime's throat closed and tears threatened at the love the siblings shared. Kevin might be frustrated, but it didn't diminish the love he held for Bethany. How she wished she'd had the same kind of relationship with her sister. When she married Kevin, she'd be gaining a new one. *Maybe I can have something like that with Bethany.* She hoped so.

She'd be gaining a family who cared about the disparate members and would leave no one behind. Not just the SEALs from Beta Squad, but also Bethany and Mack McMacken. They wouldn't give up on her, and she'd never give up on them. She'd even help them find Mack's sister if they asked.

When the siblings broke apart, Bethany clapped her hands as she grinned. "So, when's the wedding?"

"We haven't quite set a date yet because Kevin is still active in the Navy. They can go wheels-up at any time, so we're letting it ride a bit." At least in terms of the official event. As far as she was concerned, they'd sealed the deal just outside the hospital. "But you really can't tell us about what happened to you?"

Mack shrugged, spreading his hands. "Truth is stranger than fiction, especially with the SNAIFU, and they guard their secrets better than the CIA."

"We can't even show you the archaeological site in Kentucky anymore. There's a big damn oak tree in the middle of it. A tree that grew overnight according to the staff." Bethany huffed out a breath.

"Oak?" Kevin frowned. "There are no oaks in that part of the estate."

"I know, Kev." Bethany sighed and waved a hand. "Unbelievable, right?" Her gaze slid to Mack. "Weird as it may sound—and it does get weirder—it's the truth."

"Come on, it can't be that out of this world." Kevin wore an expression flatter than roadkill.

Bethany shot him her own flat look. "You have no fuckin' idea. But if you don't want to know, I can tell you we've been living here in Wyomin' for the last nine months. You can check the purchase records on the Sagittarius Wildlife Sanctuary."

Kevin growled and Jaime laid a hand on his thigh again. "How about we just hear them out a little?" She nodded to Bethany and Mack as they sat back. "Their microexpressions say they're telling the truth, at least as they believe it. Plus, they disappeared in Kentucky without a trace, and now, they live here in Wyoming, fifteen hundred miles away."

"They could've driven here."

"But that would've left a trail for me to follow." From her search, they seemed to have just reappeared here near Sundance. *How the hell did they do that?*

Kevin sighed and nodded. "Yeah. Hell yeah. I want to know everything that happened. Starting with when you left eighteen months ago."

Bethany's rueful smile curled her lips. "After Daddy informed me I'd be marrying his toady to make sure the money stayed in the family, I went for a walk with Killian. And that's when everything went from sugared shit to straight shit."

"What happened?" Jaime couldn't stop the question.

Mack tilted his head. "What do you know about the Greek myths and dimension travel?"

Jaime raised an eyebrow. "Greek myths?"

Kevin scowled. "Dimension travel?"

Mack smirked. "Oh, it gets stranger than that."

THE END

AUTHOR'S NOTE

This tale was originally written in August 2015 for Cat Johnson's Hot SEALs KindleWorld, a fan fiction program started by Amazon.com. In July 2018, Amazon cancelled the KindleWorlds program, but Cat Johnson allowed the authors who'd written for her launches to keep the connection between her characters and ours. Guardian Angel Protection Services or G.A.P.S., Rick Mann, Senator and Missy Greenwood are all characters and elements from Cat's world and are used with her permission. You can find all their books here: Hot SEALs World.

Additionally, this story is about Rimshot's search for his missing sister, but Bethany's story has already been written. You can find out about Bethany and Mack's adventure in TAKE THE REINS, Book One in the Rifts Series. It's even more wild than they've alluded to here.

Siobhan

TAKE THE REINS
RIFTS, BOOK 1
SNEEK PEEK

Social change is normal for a senator's daughter, but affecting gender politics in centaurs wasn't on Bethany's agenda.

All Bethany Stanton needed was time away to think. She never imagined a walk with her horse might lead her so far from home. When she steps through a rift between worlds at an old archaeological site, she realizes she has bigger problems than marriage to the man of her nightmares. Like a herd of centaurs with distressing views on gender equality and "mythical" humans.

As part of the Supernatural Anomalies Investigative Field Unit, Major Stephen "Mack" McMacken has seen and done more weird stuff than written in a science fiction novel. When called in to track down a U.S. Senator's missing daughter, Mack figures it's more a case of runaway rich girl than supernatural mystery. Until his team finds the portal and he's nearly torched by a dying phoenix.

In a world ruled by mythical beasts, Mack and Bethany find themselves on trial for endangering the centaur village. With the only escape route they know gone, working together to establish their innocence might prove easier than avoiding seductive Sirens and ravenous native beasts.

And then there's the not-so-simple matter of finding a way back home…

BAM-BAM'S INKED HART
BAD BOYS OF BETA SQUAD, BOOK 3
SNEEK PEEK

Petty Officer Greg "Bam-Bam" Killian is done with marriage, done with long term relationships, and done with the Teams. The injury sustained on his last op has destroyed his dreams of being a SEAL as much as his ex-wife demolished their marriage. Now he's free to do anything he wants, including get drunk and be miserable.

Zamora Hart has dealt with her fair share of men, both military and civilian. When a wounded petty officer washes up in her tattoo shop, she can't help but offer him a place to stay for the weekend. She's been where he is and doesn't mind paying the help forward, especially when the friendship comes with some intimate benefits. It's only temporary.

When Zamora's ex shows up, frightening her with talk of starting over, Greg offers to stay at her place longer to give backup and repay her generosity. He doesn't intend to fall in love with her, he's only defending a friend while he shifts his career from active service to BUD/S instructor. But her ex's threats become more than just talk, and Greg must step up his efforts of protection, because that's what friends do.

But it's only temporary and they're just friends-with-benefits, right?

OTHER BOOKS BY SIOBHAN MUIR

Queen Bitch of the Callowwood Pack

Cloudburst Colorado Series
A Hell Hound's Fire
The Beltane Witch
Christmas I.C.E. Magic
Cloudburst Ice Magic
Cloudburst Coffee & Spa

Rifts Series
Take the Reins
A Centaur's Solstice Wish
In Death's Shadow

Bad Boys of Beta Squad Series
Bronco's Rough Ride
The Navy's Ghost
Rimshot's Hard Target
Bam-Bam's Inked Hart
Deli's Take Out

The Ivory Road Serial
A Walk in the Sand
Outback Dreams

Triple Star Ranch Series
Rope a Falling Star
Star Light, Star Bright

Warbler Peninsula Series
Order of the Dragon
The Valkyrie's Sword
Burning Yuletide

Second Chance Succubus (Capitol of Second Chances #1)
Darwin's Evolution (Ultimate Recon #1)
Wildfire's Heart (Elemental Hearts #1)
Her Devoted Vampire

Coming Soon
My Forever Cocky Biker Encounter (Concrete Angels MC #1)
Dude With a Cool Car (Concrete Angels MC #2)
Angel Ink (Concrete Angels MC #3)

ABOUT THE AUTHOR

Siobhan Muir lives in Cheyenne, Wyoming, with her husband, two daughters, and a vegetarian cat she swears is a shape-shifter, though he's never shifted when she can see him. When not writing, she can be found looking down a microscope at fossil fox teeth, pursuing her other love, paleontology. An avid reader of science fiction/fantasy, her husband gave her a paranormal romance for Christmas one year, and she was hooked for good.

In previous lives, Siobhan has been an actor at the Colorado Renaissance Festival, a field geologist in the Aleutian Islands, and restored inter-planetary imagery at the USGS. She's hiked to the top of Mount St. Helens and to the bottom of Meteor Crater.

Siobhan writes kick-ass adventure with hot sex for men and women to enjoy. She believes in happily ever after, redemption, and communication, all of which you will find in her paranormal romance stories.

Connect with Siobhan online at:
https://www.siobhanmuir.com
https://www.siobhanmuir.com/siobhans-blog
https://twitter.com/SiobhanMuir
http://pinterest.com/siobhanmuir.35
https://www.facebook.com/siobhan.muir.35